## DATE DUE

THIS
FULL
HOUSE

VIRGINIA EUWER WOLFF

# THIS
# FULL
# HOUSE

THE BOWEN PRESS

**HARPER TEEN**

*An Imprint of HarperCollins Publishers*

HarperTeen is an imprint of HarperCollins Publishers.

Library of Congress Cataloging-in-Publication Data
Wolff, Virginia Euwer.
This full house / Virginia Euwer Wolff. — 1st ed.
    p. cm.
Summary: High-school-senior LaVaughn's perceptions and expectations of
her life begin to change as she learns about the many unexpected connections
between the people she loves best.
ISBN 978-0-06-158304-9 (trade bdg.) — ISBN 978-0-06-158305-6 (lib bdg.)
[1. Novels in verse. 2. Conduct of life—Fiction. 3. Best friends—Fiction.
4. Friendship—Fiction. 5. Interpersonal relations—Fiction. 6. High schools—
Fiction. 7. Schools—Fiction.] I. Title.
PZ7.5.W65Th 2009                                    2008020157
[Fic]—dc22                                                CIP
                                                              AC

Typography by Andrea Vandergrift
1  2  3  4  5  6  7  8  9  10
❖
First Edition

for Max Hamel

# Acknowledgments

Thanks to: Elizabeth Harding; Anthony Wolff; Juliet Wolff; Sarah Hamel; SuEllen Pommier, Ph.D.; Beth Stebbins, CNM; Naomi Shihab Nye; Gene and Meg Euwer; Madison Macht, M.D.; Marlow Macht, M.D.; Glenda Quan, M.D.; Randall Coleman, M.D.; Kori Anderson, R.N.; Joe Croft, R.N.; Jill Bayne, R.N.; Martha Goetsch, M.D.; Grace Chien, M.D.; Monique Johnson, Ph.D.; Sue Richards, Ph.D.; Constance Jackson, M.D.; Michael Lemmers, M.D.; Virgie Daigle; Kathy Scopacasa; Elizabeth O'Connor; John Melville; Lawson Fusao Inada; Mary Gunesch; Gregory Maguire; Sonya Sones; Lisa DeGrace, Helen Townes, Sue Knight, Rosa Hemphill, Bill Lamb, Pam Dreisin, Rob Brisk, and Margaret Kahl of Oregon Episcopal School; Jamie Kelso and Becky Fariss and their biology students at West Linn High School; Kate Fisher and her advanced biology students at Oregon City High School; Laurie LePore and her ninth-grade genetics class at Riverdale High School, especially Zeno L'Hericy and Alex Hess, my lab partners; Patrick Stauffer and Zoe Ros; my readers' theatre colleagues David Almond, Cornelia Funke, Tim Wynne-Jones, and Elizabeth Poe; the staff of the Gladstone Public Library; and, muscle and sinew, to Brenda Bowen. And especial gratitude to the late Marilyn E. Marlow.

THIS
FULL
HOUSE

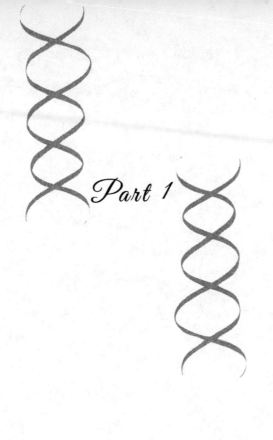

Part 1

## 1.

I could not have known.
Would never have predicted.
As if I had been a leaf floating in a gutter toward the sea
or a puff of dust blowing through an open window.

That was how much I knew
about how this would all happen
how we would all end up.
No more than that.

## 2.

Jilly and Jeremy come scurrying
from the swings,
scuttling up little whirls of dirt,
hopping and smiling, such energy of pep and joy
and it's only a bag two-thirds full of popcorn
I'm holding open in my hand.

Jeremy is transformed into a big kindergarten boy,
consuming books so fast he has to read them over and over
before Jolly can take him back to the library
between her school and work hours.
Jolly, who did not have such a thing as a library card
till this amazing boy turned out to be
such a bookish child
and who also appears to be Batman at times
as well as other flying people.
Jilly herself is nearly four,
friendly as always,
she likes to play cards
because the King and Queen
and their Jokester amuse her.
She imitates their faces

2

and waits till we notice
before she puts her own face back on.

Jolly goes to school to get her G.E.D.,
Jeremy prints huge words in kindergarten
like CATFISH and FROG and POCKET,
way oversize in his nearsighted vision.
And Jilly makes blobs of clay into different blobs of clay
bending over her work like a sculptor in Head Start
so she will have a head start.
She is in the same building I was,
back when Myrtle and Annie and I were so little
and the teachers nailed our coathooks on the wall
down where my knees are now.
Those same coathooks are still there,
Jilly's coat goes
where Annie's little red one used to hang,
I would recognize that red a block away,
as I used to,
Annie coming along skipping on squares,
avoiding the cracks in the sidewalk,
jouncing her mama's arm till it would nearly fall off,
her mama said.

And I believed her. I told my mom,
"Annie's mama's arm gonna fall off,"

and my mom told me that was plain foolishness,
no small child could break off a part of a mother.
I was finding out how moms are indestructible.
And sometimes I think my mom is the only one
who still is.

Jilly leaps into the classroom in the morning,
scoops sand at the sand table, pouring it back and forth,
paints big pink and yellow paintings at the easel,
loves to sit on teachers' laps.

This little one who wouldn't have been born
if boys had been nice to Jolly,
and who would be dead now
if Jolly had not blown life back into her.
This child can give champion hugs
and go in the potty like a big girl.
She sleeps with a book, lying on top of it.
Sometimes it's a book about scooters,
sometimes it's *Goodnight Moon*,
and she recites them at any time of day.
Jilly runs to me in this shiny afternoon
with her arms outstretched
and Jeremy is planted in front of me, the giant
at the top of the beanstalk.
He scares us with "Fee! Fi! Fo! Fum!"

in his small child roar
and reaches his giant hand into the bag for popcorn.

Jilly noses the bag, chirping, "Tweet, tweet,"
her nose a beak, her eyes bird's eyes.
Tree branches weave waves of light on their faces.

We leave the playground
hand in hand in hand,
skipping, loping, galumphing,
being rabbits and giraffes and hippos,
and by the time we get to Jolly's house
I am ready to drop.

## 3.

Jolly made soup.
She soaked the beans, boiled a chicken for broth,
she sliced up carrots, celery,
started at the top of the onion,
leaving the root end for last
in order to cut it without crying.
She tore the slippery chicken meat off the bones
and slid the pieces into the pot
that Ricky brought home from the Goodwill.
She remembered to keep the heat on low
so the soup wouldn't burn,
I watched her stirring it all together, doing this task
that she never did before.
In her whole congested apartment
the air steamed with vegetables,
drawers were not hanging open,
chairs were right side up, waiting.

Such a thing as making soup:
Not once did she threaten to quit in the middle
as I have seen her do
with other things.

Jeremy helped set the table,
putting out spoons for everyone.
I tore paper towels from the roll
and he put one on the table for each of us five,
with Ricky home in time for supper.

Jilly and I had a hairbrush situation
when she started to pick up Jolly's
"private personal hairbrush and don't you *ever* forget it."
I shooshed Jilly away
and steered her toward her own.
I whispered to her
how she always has to use her own brush,
which she already knew, of course.
She sparkled her eyes up at me,
this huggable child.

Everybody ate up this good soup,
Jilly slopping it in front and to the side
and saying, "Jewemy says octopus gots no bones?"
looking around
to see if we will help her catch Jeremy being wrong.
Ricky says, "He's right, Jilly. Remember the aquarium,
the octopus goes all squished? He couldn't do that
if he had bones."

Jeremy counts the pieces in his bowl
and reports to his mother:
"There's 2 carrots
and 4 green things, 5-6-7 brown pieces,
and slippy ones
and two chickens."

This is Jolly who got so thrown down
in her poor life
and nobody saved her
so she is figuring out
how to save herself.

"You keep on with school,
you'll learn things too
like Mommy learned to make soup," says Ricky
down to Jeremy who concentrates on him
from inside his new glasses
with doggies on their frames.
A child in kindergarten fell down on his other ones.
Jeremy is such a good sport
about wearing his thick glasses;
he has worn them since he was not yet even three.

Everyone in this room goes to school.
Even Ricky, who got accepted for Firefighter Training,

which makes Jeremy worship him. Jeremy sings:
"I'm a fireman fighter with my own boots on,
they gots handles to put on with,
they gots handles to put on with."

Jolly who says she never had any folks at all,
a throwaway child
who won't even answer questions
about when she was little:
Now her own son is in kindergarten
and he can read and count.
He keeps a total of cockroaches he sees in a day,
then he starts over again the next morning.
Sometimes when we meet he shouts,
"Fourteen, LaVaughn!"

And Ricky has not left Jolly yet.
The only one who didn't, I guess.
Once when Jolly got storming mad at everything
she hollered, "Why don't you just go?
Everybody else done that,
how come you ain't left yet?"
And Ricky said back to her,
"It wouldn't be the right thing to do."
Jolly asked me,
"LaVaughn, you ever think any guy ever said to me

about 'the right thing to do' before in my life?
Never, not ever, not one,
not till Ricky."

I keep wondering
how all this can be, and I want to sing out:

*Hey, everybody,*
*look at Jolly! Look how she does her life!*
*Could you do that?*

Instead I tell her in a blunt, unimportant voice,
"This soup is excellent, Jolly.
You're good!" She looks at me,
her eyes coming from underneath
and sideways,
admitting and yet not admitting that she's good,
and I could jump with happiness.
I do not.
I eat a second bowl of soup and listen to Jilly
telling me about the world.
"Octopus gots no bones," says Jilly.
A piece of celery tips off her spoon onto my arm.

# 4.

When I first met Jilly
she couldn't have imagined an octopus
and I was merely 14.
What did I know?
Almost nothing.

Back then I barely had twinges of growing up,
and now I can be mature for hours at a time.
It just takes willpower.
I am now so advanced
I am nearly splitting through my skin
with impatience
to grow completely up and do
things I don't even know the names of.
Science things,
a real job.
Well, and have love, too.

## 5.

After the soup I go home from Jolly's,
7 stops on the Number 4 bus
as I have done for years.

Would I have made that first trip
if I had known?
If I'd seen ahead
that it would take me to their house
and their bad luck
and awful complications that happened to everybody
in such variety?

If I had known
how it would make me look for a different job next time
and get in with the sick children
and how I got so sure I would not have Jolly's bad luck
and I had my own horrible luck,
nearly falling down blind
with what were only everyday facts
but they knocked me out,
and I am standing upright again—

Would I have taken that first bus ride?
I pull the cord for my stop.
The driver knows me and says, "LaVaughn,
you getting tall or you just getting old?"
I laugh and swing myself and my backpack
down the steps.

## 6.

The struggling ache in me
is to be in charge of something.
All my life I have asked people:
Can I do this?
Why can't I do that?
Should I do the other thing?
Who will show me how to do
all these things I need to do?
From learning to write my name
to finding a right after-school job
to trying to understand
why things won't go my way.

I want to be the one to say:
"This is what I'll do,
this is how I'll do it,
and now see? I've done it."

## 7.

I used to think I studied before, but it was nothing
compared with Summer Science
at the Institute way across town
where students from age 8 to 18 can go
in the summertime,
the little kids playing with colors and liquids and gears,
big ones doing chemistry and physics
and harder thinking than I ever knew existed.

In Summer Science all the equipment works:
the centrifuges, the flow cytometers,
the autoclaves, everything.
Till then I had not used a micropipette
that measured right,
had never seen a confocal microscope,
I didn't know the difference between *in vitro* and *in vivo*.
In two whole summers
when I was 16 and 17,
along with my old lab partner Patrick, too, at first,
I attended every class every day
to grow my scientific brain.

Summer Science takes up
where the closed school labs leave off.
At my regular school a whole lab is locked
from budget cuts.
It has happened in seven schools in the city
and the city leaders say it makes them sad.

Patrick & I were the next-to-last class at my school
to get to do DNA fingerprinting with agarose gels.
Not till Summer Science
did I find out the new way: capillary electrophoresis,
and I can say those big words and more.
I even know Kary Mullis won a Nobel Prize
for inventing the polymerase chain reaction, PCR,
I got the whole thing right on a quiz.

From Summer Science I can recite
many parts of the periodic table,
invented by the Russian chemist
Dmitri Mendeleev in 1869.
He figured out atomic weights of elements,
and he left gaps and question marks in his table
because he knew he hadn't discovered everything.
"Never assume you know all there is to know,"
said our teacher, who's really a college professor

doing this for free
because he feels sorry for kids without lab classes.
"Be like Mendeleev—
always leave gaps
for what someone else will discover later.
We know so little. . . ."

And we studied so many things
large and small:
stress reaction in zebras,
the hippocampus of rats.
I made a scrapbook of artiodactyls and gave it to Jeremy.
Jilly tore out the warthog page and hid it under her pillow.

Startling animal facts:
The arctic tern flies 21,000 miles each year in migration.
Even fungus spores can travel 4,000 miles across oceans.
Brown rats need two ounces of water daily
and their bite can exert a pressure
of 7,000 pounds per square inch.
A red blood cell is one-thousandth the size of an ant.
Female spotted hyenas are just as aggressive as males.
Human beings have the same size brain
they had 150,000 years ago.

We saw Venus and Jupiter and its moons at night
through a huge telescope
and spent a whole week on eyes.
Eyes of different species, different refractions.

I had never heard of Niels Bohr
and his Nobel Prize for physics.
("Why in the world not?"
said one student, turning around in her chair
and looking at my clothes.
I said, "I don't know," and she looked away from me,
going back to her perfect notebook
with marginal notes on both sides of the page.
I admit her look has come back to me at odd times.)
Neils Bohr has hydrogen orbits named after him.

In fact, here is what I copied from that girl:
how to divide every notebook page into three columns,
wide in the middle and a narrow one on each side.
On the left go major headings,
which I can put in later
if I can't figure them out right away,
and on the right are things I don't catch on to.
The middle is for the regular notes.
My right-hand side is always full
of question marks and arrows.

Not all of Summer Science was exciting; sometimes it was
just plain hard work, measuring and making mistakes
and measuring again
and worrying that I've put the decimal point
in the wrong place in my lab notes
and often I did.

Would you like to know
the melting point of aluminum, atomic number 13?
660.37° Celsius. That decimal point is correct.

We learned that in the 4th century BCE, Aristotle
thought parents carried traits to their children
through their blood.
And there was the monk Gregor Mendel
and his peas in Austria in the 1800s.
We studied how he counted
the purple and white pea flowers
and experimented with them for eight years,
how he kept getting more purple flowers than white ones,
and he called the inherited traits "particles of inheritance."
He even thought up "dominant" and "recessive,"
but the other scientists
didn't even bother to say "Oh!" or "Hmm."
And then he died.

On Skit Day we all got to be scientists in costume
and I played Gregor Mendel.
They found me a monk's robe and I had pea plants
and I made a diagram
showing the dominant and recessive traits
in A's and a's just the way Mendel figured them out.
In his time, nobody had heard of restriction enzymes
or plasmid DNA
but now in our modern century
we can see the chromosome banding patterns
because of him and his peas in the 1860s.

The girl with the notebook acted out Niels Bohr.
"Every sentence I utter must be understood as a question,"
she said, in a man's suit and a deep voice.
"This is what I want to be remembered by."
A crater on the moon is named after this man
and he wanted to be remembered as a question mark.

Even when it was too hot
for people in their right minds
to get on two buses to go to the Institute
and splurge their energy on study, I went there.
Sometimes only because I had promised myself I would.

We went to three oozing swamps,
we collected water in jars
and went back and analyzed it.
Small creatures live in that toxic water despite everything,
and mutations happen.
Living creatures adapt, that's the lesson we kept learning.

On one of our swamp trips
we each had four children with us,
nine-year-old Summer Science kids,
and we helped them decide on a project and do it.
My team found three frogs
and drew them in their notebooks,
drawing fast while I held each one in a net,
dipping it in water and lifting it out again,
the surprised frogs, the steady pulsing of their throats,
beautiful amphibians in a beautiful place
full of horrifying invisible poisons. These small children
are the ones who can be good students
without much effort
because of the excitable axons and dendrites
in their brains,
their neuroplasticity. Two days of brain science
explained that to me.

My team partner and I taught some 11-year-olds
how to extract the DNA of a kiwifruit
and the professor said her high praise,
"Good job, good job."
Well, someone *might* ask those children someday,
"How do you extract DNA from a kiwifruit?"
And they will be ready.

## 8.

My old lab partner Patrick
won the Summer Science Prize
with his project about a disease I had never heard of,
hepatolenticular degeneration,
that comes from an autosomal recessive defect
on chromosome 13, gene ATP7B,
and means that the person
has accumulated copper in the tissues.

("Well, it's just— There was this twitchy guy
in one of the places I lived,
and I just kind of wondered."
So he investigated chromosome 13. I do not know
others who would do this for such a reason
as twitchiness in a person at a foster home.)
And he won another prize
for the moons of Saturn skit he did with little kids
who danced in a circle and sang the moon names,
"Titan, Rhea, Mimas, Dione . . ."
their small feet and voices making music
till the whole audience sang along.

In fact, he was everywhere.
Just when I thought he was in Molecular Biology
he was suddenly in Astronomy, too,
and then he did a Geology project about shocked quartz
after underground nuclear bomb testing.

Patrick and I ate lunch together at the Institute.
"A giraffe's heart weighs 25 pounds, LaVaughn,
can you imagine that?" always in his slow sentences,
always with his studious eyes.
Having such huge facts
seems to steady his running mind.
He estimated the weight of the French fries in grams,
and built impossible structures
with the plates, cups, glasses, and straws
till everybody in the cafeteria would come to watch,
hanging silently while his plastic towers grew,
then the closest watchers would reach out
to catch a falling piece.
Everyone in Summer Science knew who he was,
his peaceful voice, his calm hands.

Even before he won the prizes
the teachers were talking about him,
this same boy
who respected every tiniest kind of animal or mineral

back when he was my lab partner,
the boy who held the test tubes
while I tried to keep the pipette from wobbling.

And then suddenly he changed schools,
got taken away to the Academy of the City,
a new school in an old building
for all very smart people.
They wear uniforms and have excellent lab classes
and their own science in summer,
with field trips to far places,
deserts and astronomy observatories.
Patrick disappeared into that school, poof.

And I never found out if he forgave me
for being mean and childish and not noticing I was,
way long before we ever heard of Summer Science.
His quiet face did not show any detail of this,
not even during all those lunches
and now he's gone. He barely said Goodbye.

His fingerprints are in labs, on doorknobs,
his hand motions hang in that sterilized air,
people say they miss him.

## 9.

As a reward for going every day to Summer Science
my mom got me a good study lamp for my desk,
and it cost her one whole entire day's wages at her job
and she did it anyway.
About this woman my mom,
I could complain a list 40 items long
but then she does those things: a lamp she can't afford.
My complaint list would do no good at all.
I am probably not
the perfect daughter she always wanted either.

# 10.

Summer Science is long gone,
the weather is cold
and here is how the day goes:
5:10 a.m. Alarm rings.
Between 5:18 and 5:22 a.m.
my mom knocks on my door to make sure.
5:28 a.m. I am in the shower, steamy from my mom
who has just stepped out of it.
I "eat a healthy breakfast or else,"
my mom's lifetime rule.
7:00 a.m. I am at a computer in the library at school,
third row, third station from the left,
doing whatever assignment is most urgent for the day
if the computer system is working that morning.
It is my regular time each morning except Thursday
when I have the College Fact meeting,
with about eleven other people
who also want to go to more school after high school.
We have all taken the big tests
and have seen our scores
which the College Fact advisor tries to comfort us about.

"No, these are not *bad* scores," she says,
trying to look happier than she feels.

When I sit at the computer
the librarian whose job they keep threatening to cut
comes along behind me
and says, "LaVaughn, you're one determined girl."

I go through my classes
where the teachers try to get their voices heard.
Some students sit on the radiators
because chairs are broken or missing,
some kids are napping or being rude,
but I write the page numbers assigned
and I make sure I get a book
even when we have to share.

Then I go up to the Children's Hospital
to fold laundry
and visit the little sick kids there,
some of them have such horrible things,
I have known two who have died,
but my little friend Lee Anne
got her bone marrow transplant
and is not in the hospital anymore.

Her mother mails me letters at the nurses' station
with drawings that Lee Anne has made for me.
I have three of them on my bedroom wall,
a dog, a garden, and a horse,
above the photograph of my dad and me
in matching baseball caps.

While I fold laundry I memorize things for school,
dates of wars:
French ones, African ones, Russian ones,
battles of all ugly kinds.
It's a shame to have us hopeful young students
learn these horrible things.
Exactly the kind of behaving
they have told us over and over again not to do
is what the history class is full of,
full-grown adults making these wars:
killing each other for land, for religions,
for greed and more greed.
Why bother to have children and educate them
and invent things to make their lives better,
just to send them off to war to get slaughtered?
That is my opinion.

At 5:30 p.m. I check out of the hospital

and just inside the door to the outside world
I open my books to remind me
what I should be memorizing on the bus home.

I walk to the bus stop reciting war facts.
On the bus I study peace treaties.
I walk in the door at home
where I can smell a good supper
and my mom is talking on the phone
about the Tenant Council rotations
and stirring supper with one hand
while she writes something
on her Safety Patrol bulletin board with the other.
She is changed out of her good work clothes
from the office
into old relaxy things, she waves to me
and out from the fridge come ingredients for salad,
which is my job to concoct.

We have supper.
She asks questions. "What's your hardest thing
for homework?"
I tell her: Some political war.
She shakes her head at human evil.
She asks what the next hardest is.

I draw the sines and cosines and tangents
of a triangle
and I begin to explain their ratios
and before I have gone very far with it
she holds her fork in the air with healthy supper on it
and says, "LaVaughn. I never. I just never.
You *know* those things?"
"Yeah, I do," I say, and I admit I am proud.
"Well. I never," she says again,
and we finish supper with how her day went at work.


She has never missed a day of a job,
I have never missed a day of school,
even that one I threatened to miss
two years ago, when my heart and mind were collapsed,
flattened, deep in hiding from the light of day.
Chocolate chip cookies: I had baked them,
including nuts and grated orange rind,
I took them as a get-well present. I opened the door
I saw Jody in a kiss,
which said for sure
he would never kiss me.
The story of my life dropped out from under me.

I went to every one of my classes
and it was because of this mom I have
who forced me to.

It's hard, this way of life, but it's what we've got.

## 11.

And when I look back into my life like an X-ray:
Jody.

For months I practiced thinking his name
in a steady voice,
the way I would mumble names of other boys,
I practiced pretending he is just anybody.

I got so I could say that word out loud.
Jo dy.
It had lain bending, stretching in my mouth
for such a long time,
and one day
I found I could say it without quivering.

You might think, "It's just a word, only a name."
And you would be wrong.
Not just, not only. It took me months.

When I could finally say his name
I got the courage to tell my friend Ronell
about that plate of cookies,
that day I thought was the end of my life.

She listened, she squinched her mouth around,
she paid attention.
She said, "You won't make that same mistake again."
This was not quite comforting.
"You'll make different ones, come on, LaVaughn,
we all will.
You are not alone."
There was a boyfriend in her life history
who lied about everything, even his name.
"I couldn't imagine it, either, till it happened.
We don't just stop living, do we?" she says.
Ronell is right: I am walking around.
I'm not dead of it,
and won't be.


And I will say this about my mom:
She understands why I cannot face a chocolate chip,
can't even look at the package.
Having such a mom
is good luck. I could have gotten one
who would not bother to understand.


The worst thing:
Jody's locker door had scary graffiti
written on it,
**YOU ARE GONE** in giant, messy letters,

and everybody who walked past saw it,
and I wanted to sink through the floor.
When I saw Jody and two other kids
cleaning it off with toothpaste
I tried to help
but there wasn't room
so I walked away
angry enough to scream.

Three days later,
more graffiti. This time it said **FILTH**.
Of course my brain raged.
I used toothpaste from my own backpack,
but it is slow work
and I didn't get finished before the bell rang.

The next week Jody's locker door
got bashed in
with a baseball bat or something
and two people got kicked out of school for five days.
I don't know who they were and I don't want to.
I heard people saying "outside influence."
I wanted to know
but closed my ears to it all.

Sometimes life is just too horrible.

I went and shot baskets with three other people
I didn't even know,
at the end of the gym
where the basket hasn't been pulled
off the backboard yet.

Jo dy.
Still the most beautiful boy I ever saw.

## 12.

I envy Patrick's brainy Academy:
The students are treated like royalty
but they have iron-strict rules.

Their uniforms have to be perfect
as well as their fingernails.
Everybody stands up
when a teacher comes into the room,
their principal who knows the name of everyone
and says Good Morning to each student
in their different languages.
They have tutorials and seminars
and even the bathroom signs are in Latin words.

Patrick and I were on the same bus once,
standing and hanging on to the metal bar
even though our schools are far apart.
He came up to me from the back,
and asked me if I was still LaVaughn.
I was happier to hear his soft, slow voice
than I thought I would be.

When I turned and looked up to his face
it was the same face I had hurt so long ago,
this Patrick who was nice to me
but who could not have forgotten
I had been mean, so mean.

He is taller now.
We swung as the bus swayed
and we said brief things to each other,
fumbling,
and that old Summer Science feeling
wouldn't or couldn't come back.

I asked him about his new school.
He told me about the uniforms, the fingernails,
the standing up for teachers coming into rooms.
The Latin. And the labs. He says
one of his teachers found a new enzyme.
"Can you imagine, LaVaughn?
Nobody knew about it before. . . ."

This is my old lab partner,
who used to have two sweatshirts
and went to my old crumbling school.
I don't change my face.

"So when we went to the U. for the genetics lab . . ."

"To the what?" I ask him.

"The U., the university.
We get to use their genetic analyzer,
their scanning electron microscope,
their biosensors—
you could go over there with me sometime,
I've got a card now."

These are just words he's saying
but they shush me right up:
Patrick and his brain are now so promoted,
in some ways he's unrecognizable,
but his hand holds his bus pass the same old way.
I don't know what to answer.
The other time he invited me to something
I was rude and not honest
and I would like to untangle that,
make myself not the girl who did that,
but instead I say, "Scanning electron microscope?"
What I meant was
       *How did you get so far away from the way*
       *we used to be?*
       *You're so way ahead of me I can't even apologize now*

*and don't you know*

    *how sorry I am about being mean two years ago?*
"Well, yeah. You should see it. It can magnify
200,000 times. The fruit flies look like Martians,
the ants have rounded armor—
it's a vacuum inside so they have to be dried
and then coated with a thin layer of gold—
it's done with electrons—"

I look up at his excitement.
"The ant's head is less than half a millimeter long,
and we can see it this big."
He holds his fingers about eight centimeters apart.
Now his fingers are familiar again,
how they used to work on our experiments together,
how I got so used to them
I would recognize them anywhere,
even though I thought I had forgotten them.

His hands used to stick out of the raggedy sleeves
of a sweatshirt,
and now he wears a white shirt, necktie,
dark blue blazer,
studies microorganisms and ant faces
and doesn't look like my neighborhood.
He says more science before I get off the bus:

"LaVaughn, can you imagine:
A roundworm has 19,000 genes.
A mustard plant has got 25,000.
With the genetic analyzer,
the sequences of anything—anything—
show up on the computer screen—"
Why doesn't he ask anything about me?
I've got genes, too—

Then he says,
"How are you, LaVaughn? How's school?"
I don't know what to say.
School is the same,
but with the science labs closed down
and the gym roof leaking
and too many people angry and exhausted.
I say school is okay. My mind is not on that.

Seeing Patrick on the bus that way
agitated my afternoon.
At home I got grouchy for no reason,
I threw a fork into the sink,
I sulked.

In the mirror was not a nice face,
the face of a pouter, a sulker,

bad company for myself.
Patrick with his card for the U.,
he gets to walk right in
wearing his fancy school uniform,
looking almost like a college person.
I threw my hairbrush into the bathtub, hard.

And then I had to scour the scar it made,
so my mom wouldn't know
I had done such a childish thing
and all the time a lump in my throat
getting in the way of every thought.

Patrick and his lofty brain.
Me and my lowly one.

## 13.

I take Jeremy and Jilly home with me one afternoon
when Jolly has her study group.
We stop at the Goodwill near my house
so they can each pick out a book.
These children judge a book by its cover,
Jeremy gets a thick one about insects
and Jilly chooses one because it's red.
They are good walkers by now, these two,
and we hike home from the store.
Jilly takes off her coat in the sunshine.

She runs toward a pigeon,
waving her coat open toward it.
"I warm that buhdie," she shrieks.
Naturally, the bird takes off, terrified.

"That bird ain't cold," says Jeremy.
"Jeremy, you can't say 'ain't,'" I tell him.
"You've gotta say 'That bird isn't cold.'
Get it?"

"He gots feathers, they insultate him,
he ain't cold, I tell you, Jilly!"
Jilly is watching where the bird flew away,
high on a building ledge.
"Way high up aoh," she points.

"And the word is 'insulate,' Jeremy," I say.
"How do you know that? About feathers
and insulation?"

Jeremy reaches in his pocket
and pulls out a broken wheel from some toy.
He rolls it around in his hand.
"Everybody knows that," he says.

No, everybody does not know that.
This Jeremy surprises me every time I see him.

At my house we read Jeremy's new book
and find out that the wings of a housefly
beat 200 times per second
and that the fly doesn't grow.
It is born full size.
This fly has 4,000 lenses in each eye
and it jumps up and backward

when it takes off into the air.
Flies smell with their antennae.

Even a whole week later,
Jeremy is telling me these things.
"Four million lenses in his eyes!"
I remind him that it's four thousand,
and this is not enough difference to disappoint him.
Kids and their synapses.
They're spine-tingling.

## 14.

And then the Guidance Office called me in.
I know every chair,
the names of the changing secretaries,
and have been shaking hands
with the Guidance Man for years.

This time it's for a whole new thing
I never heard of before,
a thing called WIMS,
Women in Medical Science,
for girls from 16 to 20,
every Tuesday and Wednesday afternoon
through winter and spring,
to get girls ready to do science in college
and maybe even nursing for me.
45 girls from poor schools in the whole city
get in each year
because of rich people and a foundation
and there are waiting lists.
"We will send your grades.
And your Summer Science evaluations,
I notice they're very good,

your professors liked your dependability.
You must do the rest, LaVaughn.
The qualifying test is on Thursday," says the Guidance Man,
"and then you'll be given an appointment for the interview."

"What do I—" I start, and he stops me
with his hand up
like a sign. "Think about what you've learned
in Summer Science, and from Dr. Rose,
and bring your reasoning ability with you.
And get a good night's sleep on Wednesday."
He puts the application and the test admission ticket
in my hand.

I do what he says but not without shaking,
worrying, telling myself not to worry,
and waking up with worry
at least three times on Wednesday night.
The test is short,
with some chemical equations,
some math problems,
and one writing question.
"Discuss an instance in your life when you have used
patience, tolerance, flexibility, and persistence
in solving a difficult problem."
My mind went blank, of course.

The College Fact meetings have taught me
to swim through the blankness
and grab on to the touchable items that I can't see at first.
I swam through it, afraid but not stopping,
and up came Jeremy's toilet training.
It would be boring to anyone who was not there,
but I wrote it down anyway.
How Jeremy denied the need for a toilet,
how I persisted, and how Jeremy caught on
but did not seem to think it was an accomplishment,
how his mother said I had stolen his toilet training
from her,
and by the time I was finished
my writing hand was sore
and I had told the whole thing.
Other girls stood up, handed in their papers,
and I did the same,
all of us silent as brooms.
I had avoided thinking about being interviewed
but now the appointment card was in my hand
and I had my choice of being afraid or not.

The card said to go up on the hill
where the hospitals are,
it's like a city up there,
where I have been paid to fold

many thousands of sheets.
I don't know what they will ask me,
and when I imagine myself in the interview
everything I know
evaporates.
One moment I know how the liver processes vitamin E,
circulating it in the blood,
and the next instant I can't remember even that.

At least I can wear the right thing.
What is the right thing?

"Don't wear yellow; it's the color of fear."
That's what my mom's friend said
as I dangled sweaters from my arms.
My mom turned her head to the side
and said, "Hmmm.
I seen very unafraid people wear yellow.
It's not a law."

"Red is aggressive. If you want to be aggressive,"
Ronell warned me. "But if you wear pink
you switch on their old-fashioned reflexes,
they think you're weak or a baby."

But then I took the Aunts shopping.

## 15.

We go grocery shopping once a week in a taxi
for their old age and slowness
and I would say this job is just as much nice as onerous.
Listen to that word! See how much I know now?
"On-er-ous." It means a heavy burden, a weight.
It's only once a week, so how onerous could it be?

Aunt LaVaughn tells the taxi driver,
"It was all nice families back then,
not but a bit of car noise,
children in the fire hydrant in summer, splashing,
it was all decent back then."
Aunt Verna looks out the window
making small noises in her mouth
about the things she sees.
A dog on the sidewalk, a building abandoned,
a tree with small leaves waving.
She's a watcher, has always been.
These women took care of my mom
for her whole childhood
till she grew up. They are my family,

wrinkled, slow to hear, sometimes grouchy,
they scrape along.

Aunt Verna at the phone company
and Aunt LaVaughn at the bakery,
they alternated their hours
so one of them could be home
when my mom got home from school.
We buy day-old bread,
reduced-price meat, blackened bananas.
Since the Great Depression
this is how they have stayed alive.

Aunt Verna has her opinion about clothing:
"Your interviewer, you want to get him to like you?
Wear blue. Always wear blue
when you want to get something from a man."
Aunt Verna took her lunch in a paper bag for 36 years,
and water from the drinking fountain
was her lunch drink,
to save money so she could buy my mom shoes.
"When I wanted a raise I wore my blue dress,
this was after the war," she says. "A nice blue dress—
it had some kind of polka dots. I got the raise every time."
She laughs and puts her elderly hand on my hand.

Aunt LaVaughn advises me:
"You'd be wearing pants? No, no, no, don't do that.
You'll wear a skirt, LaVaughn," she says.
"This is your life, you show him you're a lady,
don't mess with pants at a time like this."
The Aunts have such old things to say,
these aunts of ours have lasted well.

We put their groceries away,
we move the old canned goods to the front,
just as they've always done,
and my mom always says
I have to make sure their bathroom floor isn't icky.
I do that with a sponge.

I hug them both for thanks and love,
and I go on my way,
and they both watch down the hall
to make sure I get in the elevator
without being grabbed by a criminal.

Still, what was I going to wear to the interview?
Myrtle & Annie came to my house
and stared into my closet.
Myrtle is more interested in this clothing question
than Annie is. Annie has been away from herself

for weeks. The old Annie,
so groomed she would not let her socks be uneven,
would have given advice,
but not this Annie
who stands in my room
staring up at the birds' nest on my ceiling
as if she is not sure what a bird is.

Myrtle suggests the pale purple shirt
and the black skirt "because your aunts said no pants,"
and I think I probably agree with her,
and we decide I should wear her tan jacket on top.
It will make a better whole outfit.

So it's decided.
Now all I have to do is wait
and be jittery with nervousness.

## 16.

The interview is near where I work.
The hospitals are clustered together,
enormous buildings of several stone and brick colors
including medical school departments
with glass everywhere,
all on a hill to look down over the whole city.

This bus goes past a cemetery, thousands of graves,
all those people other people loved,
all dead under the green grass
from war and cancer and old-time childbirth.
I could wonder: "What's the use? What's the point?"
But I know this wondering does no good.
Still, even trying to be positive about everything—
about everything—everything—
birth, death, the crushing complexity in between—
It's a fact: If I am one of the 45 girls to get in,
I will ride this bus four times a week
and I will look out at the cemetery or away from it
every time I come up or down this hill,
and while I'm on my way to learn about science
all those dead ex-people will be lying there decomposing.

Riding the bus with me are medical students,
I can tell by their short lab coats and I.D. badges,
just going along like regular people.
Even doctors ride this bus with us,
in their uniform of long lab coats,
all these passengers have such brains inside their craniums,
I would think there would be a special limousine
for the very smart people,
including Patrick,
not just a public bus.
They look out the window, they see the cemetery,
they run their hands through their hair,
scratch their necks,
they use their bus passes
exactly the way I do.

From the bus stop
I walk to where I'm supposed to go,
a huge granite building
with columns like Greece or Rome.
Approaching it, my legs go noodly
and my stomach wobbles,
while I try to remember the science
I know I know.
Niels Bohr. The finches of the Galápagos.
Organic compounds contain carbon.

Lithium, beryllium, boron, carbon, nitrogen, oxygen,
fluorine, neon:
The second period of the periodic table,
atomic weights 3 through 10.
Proton donor and electron acceptor
mean the same thing: acid.
The human skeleton has 206 bones in it.
The human heart beats about 100,000 times a day.
More than that in my body this afternoon.

Up high across the front of the building
words are cut into the stone wall.
From science I know they are in the Latin language.
People had to get on very high ladders
to cut those letters,
and they would wear harnesses to keep from falling.

# SCIENTIA POTENTIA EST

The words go across the whole wall,
above gigantic columns and enormous doors.
It would mean science something.
What kind of tool did they use to cut into the stone?

I could turn around and go home. I could do that.

## 17.

I can't describe the nervous interview
where even the pictures on the walls seemed wiggly.
It is well known that you figure out later
what happened before,
because of the adrenaline and also the stomach mixup
from less blood in the digestive system
because it's going to large muscle groups,
which we needed
way back many thousands of years ago
when we were fearfully running from wild beasts.

In a hallway I remember to put a mint in my mouth
for scared breath from thinking
about how my whole future depends
on these 15 minutes.
Someone calls my name, I go through the open door,
the interviewer puts out her hand to shake
and I put mine out and I look her in the eye
and don't look away
till we are finished and she lets my hand go.
"Please sit down. That's a good handshake," she says.

I send a mental message to the Guidance Man
and listen hard for her questions.

She wants to know why I want to be in WIMS.
She wants to know if I do science in my spare time.
I say I've gone to Summer Science for two summers
and not missed a day.
I can't tell if that's a good answer or not,
I sit upright on the chair and hope.

"Your test score is quite nice.
Have you had experience in memorizing scientific data?"
I hear "Lithium 3, beryllium 4,
boron 5, carbon 6, nitrogen 7, oxygen 8 . . ."
coming out of my mouth
before I notice it is foolish and ridiculous.
I stop. She looks at me. She smiles. I don't know why.
She would not let me into the class if she knew
how many hours my mom had quizzed me
on the periodic table,
saying, "It's like I know this myself, LaVaughn,
and I don't get any of it—
The numbers look like they *should* add up—"
and how I have lain in a hot bath and cried with the effort.

Then the interviewer asks, "What is it about science
that compels your interest?"
I think about Mendel and his pea plants,
how he thought up dominant and recessive genes
and got ignored till after he was dead,
but he might not be unusual enough,
I think about the little kids and the frogs in the swamp,
none of it seems right to bring up. "I like the labs. . . ."
I say, and I know I should walk out of the room
right now
because I have failed.

I don't know why I began blurting:
"And an adult human eyeball
is 2.5 centimeters in diameter,
and a blue whale's is 15 centimeters,
and a giant squid has an eyeball that's 25 centimeters.
25 centimeters! An eyeball!"

The interviewer looked at me and nodded her head.
"Yes," she said, and then she said "Yes" again.
She did not look away from me
and I blurted again.
"Somebody goes blind every five seconds in the world.
Isn't that terrible? And once every minute a child does.

Isn't that the saddest thing?"
This was wrong, all wrong.

She said, "Your application says you want to be a nurse,
LaVern. What makes you think
you would be a good one?"
She has my name wrong.
"Uh, I've worked in the hospital for more than two years,
the Children's,
folding laundry—I mean it's only laundry, but—
uh, I've seen many little kids being sick,
with cancer, leukemia, terminal diseases—
I want— Uh, I want to help some little way—"
I rub my right hand on my skirt,
my hand is sweaty and cold,
and the interviewer says, "Thank you, LaVern,"
and even with the shakes and quivers all through me,
I tell her, "My name is LaVaughn. Please? It's LaVaughn."
Why did I put "please?" in there?

She looks quickly down at a paper
and says, "Oh— Well, thank you, LaVaughn."
She stands up, I stand up,
she shakes my hand, looking at me with a straight mouth
and I look in a straight line between her eyes
and shake back.

I walked out of the office,
through the hall to the elevator,
out of the elevator to the bus stop.
I should not have said
all those disjointed things—
a giant squid's eyeball—
Why in the world did I tell her I folded laundry?
Laundry does not take any skill.

Three medical students are standing at the bus stop
and they would have known how blithering I was,
just by looking at me. Which they did not.

The bus comes hissing to a stop, I get on,
knowing I have ended my nursing life.
I could hate myself
but for some reason I just sit in the seat,
lump lumping up in my throat,
and cry instead.

But I have no time to cry at home
because Jolly suddenly needs me
to sit the kids
while she goes to her Family Balance class.
I take my class notes
on the topic of "making peace between warring nations"

and my mom's apple cupcakes, a treat
for these little ones who keep growing while I watch.


"LaVaughn! Stop Jilly being too bolsterous!"
Jeremy hollers from their dark bedroom.
It's 8:30 at night.
My notes are spread out in the living room,
my exam is tomorrow,
I get up from the floor and walk in,
hearing Jilly humming as I go.
"Jilly, what are you doing?" I ask.


"Only humming," she says,
and her tune goes on in the dark.


"Make her stop! I can't go to sleep
with her racket."
It is not a racket and Jeremy knows this.
I reach down and pat his shoulder in the dark,
a language he is supposed to understand.
It means, "You're a big boy, be patient."


I ask Jilly, "Well, it's late,
will you stop humming
so Jeremy can go to sleep?"

She hums
and she says,
"I can't stop humming, LaVaughn,"
and she keeps on humming.

This is the child
we were afraid
was dying in front of our eyes.

"You can hum for two more minutes," I say,
and I tuck the blanket up around her.
A book falls to the floor.
I go to Jeremy's bed and touch his shoulder again.
This time it means:
"She'll drop off to sleep while she's humming."
Jeremy huffs air out his mouth without patience
to show us girls how patient he's being.
I whisper, "How many cockroaches
did you see today, Jeremy?"
He answers, "9."
"Hmmm," I say, and I kiss him goodnight again
and go back to the warring nations.

The interviewer did not want to know
the size of a giant squid's eyeball,
the warring nations will not make peace in my lifetime,

I will never be a nurse,
and Jeremy has seen nine cockroaches today.

He hollers, "LaVaughn! It was 10!
I forgot the one on the ladder!
Did you hear me? I said 10."

"That's wonderful, Jeremy. Go to sleep now,"
I say without moving,
my head full of aggressive acts of the warring nations.

"They smell with their antennas," Jeremy hollers.

"So that's how they do it," I say.
"Good night, everybody,"
and the last thing I hear
is another book falling off Jilly's bed.

Why didn't I ask Patrick
how to be in a science interview
back then when I had the chance?

## 18.

But I got in.
I got in, I got in, I got in.
I got in.
I got in. Me.
Even with the giant squid's eyeball dimensions.
I got IN!

## 19.

The first person I saw after opening the mail
was Jo dy.
Jo dy.
Two beautiful things on one autumn afternoon
made me a whirl inside that I couldn't keep up with,
and it all just rattled out of my mouth.

"Jo dy, I got accepted,
to a thing, a science thing at the hospital
after school,
I had to take a test, I had to get interviewed
and it happened, I got in. I got *in*!"

Jo dy has not gotten less beautiful
in this long time that I have tried
to keep him out of my mind.
He doesn't know I have never opened his envelope,
the one that came with the rose he gave me
that time when I surprised myself by surviving.
He secretly knows what the card said
and I secretly know I do not.
We keep these secrets

and talk around them.

"I got in!" I hear myself saying to him again.

His face goes envious for a moment.

Then he says, easily,

"Let's celebrate, then. You want to go to the Museum?"

"Huh?" I say. Jo dy has asked me to go places with him

that have sometimes included getting all wet

(the swimming pool where he trains),

falling down

(his skateboard, which I couldn't maneuver)

and shooting baskets at the playground.


I have never once said no.

"The Museum?" I say.

Jo dy is used to me not catching on.

All those months when I couldn't make my mouth work

because my heart and stomach were too dramatic

to permit human speech when I looked at him—

he used to have to wait for me to get my words out.

Such a human being:

A boy who actually waits and listens?

See why I got so crazy?


"Yeah. The Art Museum, it's just two buses."

I run upstairs and leave my pack,

fetch two apples, grab my jacket

and am back in 6 minutes,
scooting down the stairs
because the elevator is broken
(4 times since school started).

On the stairs I say to myself,
Jo dy is just another person,
just another person,
just a noth er per son,
and still, when I get to where he's waiting for me,
my heart won't stop thlunking.

But I can say his name now,
the name of this brave friend
whose locker was insulted and bashed in
and who goes on with his life.
Jo dy.

## 20.

Through the bus window
Jo dy points to some buildings with trees and a flagpole
and says it's a college.
"Huh? Where?" I point my head.
"All those buildings there.
See the huge one? That's the gym,
the pool is one whole section of it,
I swam there. It's called City University."

So that is what a college looks like.
College has been in my mind,
a castle kind of thing, floating, since I was a child.
And now here is one, just a bus ride away.
Students are on bicycles with backpacks,
I want to jump out of the bus, stop the bike riders,
see if they have three hands or larger brains
or if they are anything like me.
It has a bridge above the street
and on it in big letters in metal,
LET KNOWLEDGE SERVE THE CITY.
I gape.

"You mean that's the U.?" I ask.


"Yeah," he says and continues
about his emergency rescue training,
which comes after lifesaving at the club where he swims.
"You really ought to do it, LaVaughn,
we have paramedics teaching us—"
and he goes on about learning how to use a defibrillator
and give oxygen therapy
and the proper way to get accident victims on stretchers.
Jo dy has always wanted to save people's lives.


I watch his hands, the spread of his fingers:
He's talking about burning buildings,
people who fall from windows
or have babies in taxis. He says words:
"contusion," "contraction."
He says, "sodium levels," "ventilator," "clot."
His special course, disaster training
taught to him by instructors who want to
educate his talent.
I think of his hands lifting a fallen car door,
delivering a baby.
"You can do all that?" I ask.
"Well, I'm learning to. Yeah, I think I can do all that."

From the look on his face I think
he would do it with all his might.

We change buses,
we get to the Museum stop and jump off.
Our school I.D. cards get us in for free
"on Wednesday. Only on Wednesday," says Jo dy.
He knows where the many different rooms are,
where you go for paintings of history,
where you go to see ones of upside-down reality
"like, see? The 20th century?
Art got all different, maybe the atomic bomb,
maybe that and other things— See that one?"
It is a painting of a square. A very large square, all black.
Next to it is a square entirely green.
"See? Sometimes you wake up in the morning
and life is a black square. Or a different morning,
a green square. Or—look over here," I quickly follow him,
"see? Sometimes it's just a burlap bag filled with bones.
Get it?"
I look at the burlap bag with bones spilling out of it,
thick bones, thin ones, bones of cows and of tiny birds.
Jo dy *knows* these things
that I never thought to ask about.

He says, "Well, partly it's the way you look at it.
What do you expect
of a burlap bag of bones on the floor?
What I expect and—what they expect"
—he points to two old people across the room—
"is probably not even close.
Let's go see sculpture, OK, LaVaughn?"
I say OK, and I follow him through echoey rooms
with paintings on all sides
and up a marble staircase both wide and high,
and then to more statues than I ever even imagined
the possibility of.

Jo dy gave me that Michelangelo book that time,
and I looked all through it over and over,
and even made a project out of it in school
when I had to show something from history
that hasn't changed.

After dozens of marble people,
and birds made of brass and steel
hanging from wires high over our heads,
we come to statues made of paper,
ones made of wood and clay and feathers,
ones of sheet metal, and

then sculptures of I don't know what all,
car parts and leftover wheels from things.
"Well, life presses in on you,
tells you things, asks you things,
and if you're an artist
you keep trying to answer," says Jo dy,
and his voice echoes off a metal sheet hanging
in front of us.

I was just beginning to wonder
what these sculptures would sound like at night
if they all came to life and started arguing or singing
when we came to another huge, high room
and in the very middle of it
was a big pedestal, and on top of the pedestal
a man and a woman made of bronze
were in love, their bodies twining,
curving, bending, dark and shiny
like beautiful animals, and I just stopped and stared.
Their naked bodies were sitting down
and they were the quietest pair of people in love
I ever saw.
You couldn't not stop and stare
at these huge connected bodies.
Bronze, made of tin and copper taken from the earth,

made into human curves and muscles and lips.
And I looked through her bent leg
almost but not quite touching his bent leg,
the pyramid shape of air under their knees,
and I was in love with them.
My feelings came whooshing up
and I would have jumped up on the pedestal
and hugged them.
But my common sense came right along
and stopped me.
I could have made that leap, though.
The pedestal was not even as tall as I am.

While I was thinking about vaulting up there,
my eyes drifted under their bronze legs to the other side.
Across the room where there was—
I thought I was having a mystery moment,
not to be understood, ever,
but it was real, the whole thing was real—
There was Patrick's face
all the way across the big room,
looking right at mine.
I stood looking into his face.

He looked straight at me
and then he turned his face away
to look at another sculpture. He was with a group,
every boy wearing a necktie
every girl in a uniform skirt and jacket,
and what happened was that now I knew that I knew.

I had supposed Patrick would be back,
would walk into a class one morning
because the special school didn't work out.
The way things don't work out: It happens all the time.
It was not happening this time.
Patrick and the group
were holding notebooks in front of them
writing things down from what the guide said.
(Was Patrick getting to be in a museum art class at
that special Academy?)
And for the first time I saw
that he would never come back.
He really has gotten away,
leaving the rest of us behind.

I expected him to turn and look over his shoulder at me.
I watched him move along with his group,

farther and farther away
not looking back.


Jo dy wants to go over to a sheet of shining brass,
a bird shape with a spotlight on it.
I go with him, our shoes echo in the huge room.
He says how the sculpture flies
and stays on the earth at the same time,
and I nod my head,
I see past Jo dy's perfect profile
back into the group of students
with notebooks and attention,
the back of Patrick's head
which I used to see in biology class all the time,
especially when he would not speak to me
because I had been mean.


Jo dy and I go back home on the two buses,
we talk about things, about school,
about the art we saw.
We pass the college again,
the buildings where you could learn such smart things—
He says to choose a favorite from the Museum
and I choose the bronze lovers. But I don't say so.
I say I choose one of the hanging birds,

and I suddenly find when his sleeve touches mine
I don't go all unbalanced from head to toe.
I notice this
the way I would notice a new continent.
His sleeve is a sleeve,
and it touches mine without shaking my life.
I even try it again,
I let my sleeve brush against his
and I watch carefully:
My brain stays nearly steady.

I watch stores and offices and warehouses go by
past the bus window,
and I mostly hear Jo dy saying, "Well, looking at art
is like going to a doctor or something,
I go there when everything gets real bad."

The graffiti on his locker.
The hate words.
The bashed-in door.
I want to protect him.
I sit still
looking into my lap
and when I look up
he is pointing out how raindrops are bouncing

off the sidewalk,
and he is smiling.

Why didn't anybody ever tell me
to go to the Art Museum before?

## 21.

Standing in lunch line the next day
with about 30 people in front of me
I saw Patrick again, wearing the necktie,
his face between the bent legs
of the bronze people in love,
just his face in the air
and then it went away.

Undressing to get in the shower that night,
his face again, next to a huge bronze knee.
In a dream two weeks later,
his face against a bronze leg
but the leg was mine.
Patrick isn't going to come back
but his face and those bronze legs would not go away.

## 22.

All 45 girls get our pictures taken
on the 14th floor where we'll have our classes,
just two buildings over from where I fold laundry.

The girl who takes my registration card
is hardly older than I am. She looks at the card,
copies down a number, looks at the computer screen,
then back at me. "Verna LaVaughn. That's your name?"

I tell her yes. "But can I be mostly LaVaughn?"
Every breath I take is somewhat trembly.
She says sure, she types me in,
and in less than a minute I have my plastic badge
with my name and photograph on it.
"You'll have Dr. Moore," she says up at me.
"I never met a neurosurgeon like her,
you won't be the same after you get with her."
She goes on typing.

"How are you sure I'll have this Dr. Moore?" I ask.
"Because WIMS is her baby.
She started it,

got the funding for it by getting grants everywhere,
even convinced them to start the Foundation,
and she runs it. You'll see."

She watches me figuring out this new information.
"I was in WIMS for two years,
that's how I know, LaVaughn," she says,
looking down at her screen.
"Wait till you get in a room with her."
"How come?" I ask. Other girls are lining up behind me,
listening in.

"Well, frankly,
she's a hometown girl who made good.
She invented WIMS fifteen years ago
with just five students,"
she leans forward and lowers her voice,
"to prove a point to the board of directors.
She believes girls in this city can make it into medicine
if they get some actual support from *some*where—
like she didn't have any of.
She had to push her way past the barriers
and she believes it shouldn't be that way.
45 girls now.
You're lucky, LaVern. LaVaughn."

A woman in a short lab coat
comes around the cluster of girls
with a pile that looks like clean laundry.
She says, "She makes you want to memorize
those tons of scary data,
she makes you want to get ahead."

The pile is a stack of short lab coats,
and she begins handing them out to us.
Across the back, in big bluish-green letters,
they say WIMS.

"These coats identify you. Wear them to class each time.
And—another thing about Dr. Moore:
She smiles. She does brain surgery two days a week
*and* she still does WIMS."
This woman herself smiles around at us.
It's a smiling place.
The girl behind the counter leans forward:
"And she decides who gets into the program.
If you're in, you can be sure
she knows everything on your application."

"And could probably recite it to you,"
says the lab coat woman
and walks out through a door.

I put on the lab coat
and go into the lecture hall,
a big shiny, white auditorium
with curving rows of cushioned seats
going up higher from front to back,
and every chair has one of those side arms
where you put your book.
A bunch of us in our new lab coats
look around the room,
how it shines, how new it smells.
I don't see any chewing gum on the floor,
not a crumb of anything.
There's a huge screen,
dozens of electronic switches
and a kind of stage
where the lecture person stands
behind a thing for her papers.
One adult in a long lab coat is talking with three girls
and reading from a clipboard, smiling and smiling.
She looks generous and clear-eyed
and my knees relax some.
Dr. Moore? Not Dr. Moore?

I find a seat in the second row.
We are each carrying our shiny new WIMS binder,
red and white, and some of us are looking through it,

others are staring around the room like gulls,
watching each other, trying not to let our jitters show.
There are ballpoint-pen-clickers, foot-swingers
and I am at times both.
I am 17 years old
and I have had much practice in being shaky.

Another adult walks in with a thick binder
and thick glasses,
and she too is wearing a long lab coat,
and something comes with her,
a tone of voice although she has not spoken.

Every girl here is from a poor school
and this doctor walks in
as if we're the best roomful of students ever.
She puts the binder on the lecture stand
and smiles at every one of us,
a startling smile,
I can feel it like a beam
when it comes to me and moves along.
"WIMS.
Women in Medical Science.
These four words can connect you
with the rest of your lives, girls." Her voice.
Like a deep bell, promise, expectation.

She looks across the whole room and back again.
"Note that this is not a large group.
Forty-five, to be exact.
You are preparing to give your lives to medicine.
And what is medicine,
what do we devote ourselves to here?
Preservation of life,
restitution of health. That is our mission."
The lump in my throat comes and goes.
I think it is because
I might fail this thing.


"To my right is Dr. Faleen. I am Dr. Moore.
We wear the long coats,
we speak from this wooden lectern,
we are the connective tissue
between where you are now
and where you want to be in your future professions."
Dr. Faleen stands up, smiles and waves at us
and sits down.
Dr. Moore goes on speaking:
"Some of you will spend years giving vaccinations,
some of you will wear the goggles of research
surrounded by humming machinery in labs,
some may invent new procedures.
All of you will know more about plastic tubing

than you ever thought possible,
you are likely to become tired of microliters,
all of you will go without proper sleep.
You will memorize things
you think you cannot memorize,
facts and statistics will fly by
and you will catch them
and grow strong with the exertion.
You will find you can endure things
you thought you could not.
You will see things that shock you,
blood that sprays in your face,
you will recognize pericardial trauma
as easily as a cut finger,
you will learn why 'malignant'
is the most terrifying word in our language.
You will learn the relationship between
anticoagulants and the heart-lung machine
and you will get it right every time,
so your patients will not die under your hand.
Antibiotic-resistant bacteria will haunt you.

"Some of you will serve the poor, others the rich.
Someone will be alive because of what you did.
Someone will die because of what you could not do.
Patients will entreat you with their eyes

to make a miracle happen and stop their pain.
You will see things that will make you question why:
Why we work as we do,
why our lives are the way they are.
You will be criticized by your superiors
and you will hate some of the criticism
and want to strike back at it
and you will learn from it all."
And on the last seven words,
her smile comes again, like a greeting.
Her voice circles us together in a close loop.


And she unsmiles:
"From the discovery of the circulation of the blood
to the first open-heart surgery
to the cloning of life-forms,
medicine unfolds its mysteries in startling ways.
They are less startling to those of us
who have been paying attention.
Each discovery disturbs
the arrangements of the known world,
and it is our job to stay alert to all possibilities.
Unrestricted inquiry is our job."
She waves both arms out
toward the far corners of the room.
"The evolution of all this, all this, all of us,

when chemicals become consciousness,
appears to be a miracle
but it is not.
It is science.
That is the real wonder." She folds her hands together.

The other doctor, Dr. Faleen, says Yes with her head
and there is the silence of held breath in the rows.

"Our work demands passion,
dedication, faith.
Science is not a collection of facts,
just as music is not a collection of notes.
In science we find symmetry
and beauty and intriguing chaos.
This is not a job.
This is our calling."
She anchors her elbows on the stand
and leans out toward us.

"Girls, you must find
science irresistible.
We thrive on the exhilaration of
finding out"
—and her voice gets private and intense,
making it a secret for all 45 of us—

"*how nature works.*
If that is not your kind of exhilaration—
If you are not capable of devotion to a yeast cell—
If this is not what propels you—
Well, if it's not,
then find some other way to spend your lives."
She backs up into regular posture.
She is not smiling.


"You already know
that life takes place at the cellular level, girls.
In each human lifetime is the potential to go through
ten million billion cells.
We will spend Tuesday and Wednesday afternoons
thinking about cells
and homeostatic mechanisms
and protein chains.
We will examine the ways in which neurons
reach out to other neurons
and why.
And bones: Did I mention bones?
Be ready tomorrow afternoon."
And now she's smiling with plain good cheer.
We all shift slightly in our seats;
necks, legs, wrists budge by centimeters.
Already she has us moving together

like an organism
alert to her suggestions.

"Have you seen the inscription on this building?
See-ent-sia po-tent-sia est?"
I quick write down the way to say it
in the right-hand column of my notebook page.
"Knowledge is power, girls.
And every one of you has power.
It is our job to help you use it.
Disease and injury happen all around us;
it is natural to assume they will happen to other people.
The fine line that separates us from these other people
does not exist."

The big screen lights up
with glial cells
and by the end of the afternoon
we say "CNS" for central nervous system,
we've drawn ependymal cells in our notebooks,
we take turns explaining
the myelin sheath to each other,
and we can spell "oligodendrocyte" from memory.
This is Dr. Moore
who will change my life.

What if I'm the only one in the second row,
the only one of the 45 of us in lab coats
who doesn't have the potential?
And can Dr. Moore see that
from the lecture stand
through her thick glasses?

"Remember that healing is an honor,
and honor always means hard work.
Do not doubt that. In order to do the hard work,
you will treat your lives with the finest intelligence,
the most careful caring, girls."
She takes a breath and her smile spreads again:
"Bones tomorrow."
On our way out of the lecture hall
I notice every face I see looks just as frightened as mine.

# 23.

The next afternoon in Lab D on the 14th floor
we get bones. Nine boxes, one for each group of five girls.
"I warned you, didn't I?" says Dr. Moore,
as if we were a private club of her chosen friends.

Dr. Faleen helps us divide in teams of five,
and gets us introduced to our bones.
We must assemble our very own human skeleton,
comparing it with the model
standing in the front of the lab.
We have two weeks to finish our person.
We have to decide where to begin:
legs, arms, ribs, or where.

When she steps over to our group,
four strangers and me,
we see that she's wearing earrings of tiny photographs
of small children. Someone asks.
"Oh, these are my twins," she says, swinging her head
so the earrings shake. "I have Mother's Day every day,"
she explains. She says in an undervoice,

"They give me hope."

She announces so that all 45 of us can hear her:
"In your box are 206 bones.
This was once a human being
who cared about things and who did not live forever.
We respect these bones."
As Dr. Faleen is saying "respect these bones,"
a man in a long lab coat has walked through the doorway,
straight to Dr. Moore.
He leans down toward her, talks to her in a low voice,
his head moving with irritation,
he looks down at his watch,
pumps both hands in the air
trying to convince her of something.
We watch. Dr. Moore doesn't budge,
not even her eyelids.
She answers him,
slowly and solidly and like steel,
"This is my lab, these are my girls,
you will have to check elsewhere for a schedule revision,
no one takes this lab at 4:00 p.m. on Tuesdays
or at 4:00 p.m. on Wednesdays.
Is that clear, Claude?"

He stands completely still
for about three seconds more,
and then nods his head about four centimeters, once,
turns around and walks out the door,
his face blank.

At first we whispered it,
hesitating, in our group,
strangers till now except one girl from Summer Science.
"This is a tibia,
I know it's got to be a tibia,
look at the diagram," says one of my team.
And another one whispers down in our faces,
"Is that clear, Claude?"

Dr. Moore and Dr. Faleen
can't help hearing it
and the lab teams can't resist saying it,
it murmurs through the room.

Dr. Moore tells us the first cervical vertebra
is called the atlas, after the Greek Titan
who carried the weight of the earth on his shoulders.
We look at each other and make weighty sounds
but we are happy.

Lucky and happy with our bones.

From across the room
a girl who actually lives in Jolly's neighborhood
holds up a patella and says, "Is that clear, Claude?"
and Dr. Faleen and Dr. Moore
look at each other, trying not to laugh.

Our group gets acquainted over bones,
Naomi, Sophie, Fanta, and Shar, and I,
and we have connected seven bones wrong,
and as we disconnect them Naomi says,
"This is the *best* way to learn—by getting it wrong.
I *never* remember if I get it right the first time."
We look at our clusters of bones
and decide to name our team
"Never Right the First Time."

Riding the bus down the hill toward home
past the cemetery
bones are naturally on my mind:
The burlap bag in the Museum,
the mix of bones sliding out of it onto the floor,
our skeleton in the lab,
these decomposing bones in the cemetery.

Is it all hopeless?
We're just going to be naked bones anyway?

I shift in the bus seat, open my backpack,
take out homework and a pen.

## 24.

I have avoided telling about Annie.
Strictly made myself not tell it
because of everything. Everything.
And I'm still not ready, but it is too much not to tell.

It came to me so slowly,
I should have guessed but did not.
Back to when I got into WIMS:
"LaVaughn, you and your *groups*," Annie said.
We were always together till just two years back,
when we began dividing and it seemed so bad
but each of us knew it was not life or death.

"Groups," she said. "That Miss Rose before,
then that summer science thing,
you're always off on a bus with those books,
and now this WIMS, this wimz,
with all strangers, you
keep going in *groups*."

I didn't argue. Myrtle & Annie are my life friends.
Not "Miss Rose," it was Doctor Rose.

And Myrtle & Annie had their group, too.
We all hate the chaos it turned into
and I would not bring that up. It wasn't their fault,
that mess. Not any of it.
"Well, my name got picked. . . ."
This was the wrong thing to say.
"Well, how do you get your name picked?" said Annie.
"She scored high on tests," said Myrtle,
who I think should have stayed over there
on Annie's side,
not try to show she knows more.

This balance has always been hard,
beginning with the little wooden boat
in the Head Start room
before we could even read.
That boat could hardly balance with all three of us,
but we have always done it all these years
and it is my job to help us do it now.

"Well, I got to studying hard,
and some of the test questions were lucky ones,
and I stayed in Summer Science
and I guess the teachers there
thought I did a good job. . . ."
Annie's eyebrows aimed at these plain facts

and then she drooped, said she was tired
and just wanted to go home and take a nap.

This is not exactly the Annie I have always known.
She too was picked for something,
the Chain of Faith Disciples for their club.
They wanted her to quit school
to work full-time for them
and they would see that she got her G.E.D.
It was absurd
and Annie tried not to know that,
hooked as she was.

And after that club got so broken,
Annie, always fast on her feet,
up and joined the school jump rope squad
and Myrtle and I even turned the rope
at two tournaments.

And now Annie
wants to go to sleep.

## 25.

After their club broke up in turmoil—
and a few months went by
and Annie was jumping rope and we were cheering
and I had not yet heard of anything called WIMS—
some of the club leaders started another one,
new name and all.

This one was called Joyful Souls.
Myrtle wasn't sure at all,
she kept finding reasons not to go to the meetings.
But Annie said she felt Jesus smiling in her heart
telling her it was the right thing to do.
"It's Gary," Myrtle told me behind Annie's back.
I didn't know what she meant.
"Gary! You didn't know about Annie and Gary?"
She looked at me with reprimand but patience too.

"Myrtle, I didn't know about *any*thing in that club—
it was all a mystery."
For one, I had refused to learn anything about it.
For two, they kept it such a secret sacred thing.
For three, we had let the club twist our whole friendship,

I did it as much as they did.
Maybe more.
Yes, more.


I'll say this much: Admitting I am wrong
makes me feel so lopsided,
but not admitting is worse. That's all I know.


When the club started up again
I wasn't completely mystified,
just somewhat.
And Myrtle explained Gary.
She told me Annie and Gary had kissed, for sure.
Annie couldn't resist telling her
and Myrtle couldn't resist telling me.
Envy took over my mind.


A simple enough thing, kissing,
people do it every day. Annie is the first of us to kiss.
I kept looking at her face,
looking and looking.
Something would be different,
some kind of new thing about her.
I sometimes thought I saw it,
then it was gone.
I felt almost like a spy.

Such a private event,
I could look at her face for a week solid
and still not know.
I remember back when I hoped to have my first kiss,
I expected my face to light up or change shape,
I expected my insides to transform.

Maybe that doesn't happen.
After all, it's just lips.
It's hard to stop thinking about kissing once I start.
What is it *really* like?
But back to Gary:
He went to our school, off and on,
he was one of the Assistant Head Shepherds
in their club.
I never understood what he did for a job.
"Oh, he spreads the Lord's word," said Annie.
Her voice got shining, kind of liquid-silky.
"That's his work, he got his G.E.D.,
he is a holy pastor,
well, like a youth pastor,
that's his job."
She looks at me,
wondering whether to tell me the next part.
She decides to.
"Well, he's Major General of the Army."

"The Army?" I say. "Huh?" I missed that completely,
in thinking about how her voice got
and about how maybe the kissed thing
I was looking for in her face
was in her voice instead.

I don't say "Huh?" again. Once is enough between us
at this time.
"God's Righteous Army," she says.
Myrtle looks at her sleeve
and doesn't say anything.
"I got to be a Captain in it," Annie says.
I try to figure out how to ask:
*What does a God's Righteous Army Major General do?*
But I don't find the words.
Annie tells me, "Well, when Jesus comes in his glory
we'll get to sit on his right hand.
The trumpets and everything.
That's how come it's the Righteous Army."

Gary played the part of Jesus
in the club's play I saw two years back,
he was the star of the show,
and I remember his eyes did not seem to move.
They seemed to stay the same
whether he was blessing followers

or stamping out sins.
I really didn't notice him much,
I was just trying to watch the whole play
and didn't know the Jesus in it
was anybody in particular.

Myrtle says you wouldn't know he was special
just by looking at him,
"except he had the Lord so good and *that* made him
the best of everybody there."

He was Annie's whole life,
or so it seemed,
although I learned about it all afterward.
He said to her, "First I trust Jesus,
next I trust you, Annie," and she was convinced.

To have a boy find you like a treasure
he has been hunting for.
What would that feel like?
Gary was the whole throb of Annie's heart,
she promised she loved him
and then he stopped loving her back.
I don't know how it happened
or even when.
But suddenly Annie didn't come to school for three days,

then she was there for two days,
and stayed that way for a while,
absent for three, present for two.
It turns out Gary would show up
and her life would turn on again
just like a kitchen lightbulb.
Then he would disappear
and it would go off.

She dropped off the jump rope team.

And then the new club stopped again.
I think it wasn't a club they could count on very much.
Myrtle tells me Gary kept calling Annie
or going over to her house
when her mom wasn't home from work yet
and her sister was staying after school.

"Well, he's unpredictable" was Myrtle's explanation.
He had a bad life
with upsets of home
and he even had to go to Juvenile Court
but then when he found Jesus he repaired himself
and trusted his life to the Lord.
And he loved Annie, then he didn't,
then he did, then he didn't.

Weeks would go by and then there he'd be.
She kept his favorite cheese and crackers available
in case he turned up.
Waiting for him wore her out,
still does.
The club itself is gone
but Gary is not exactly. Not exactly.

## 26.

I am getting to it,
getting to telling about Annie.
Sometimes she and Myrtle got out their
Gospel Pal Memory Scrapbooks,
and they pored over them,
yearning for the feel of the good old days,
remembering their used-to-be excellent friends
who are mostly scattered now, drifted, gone.

"The club should of held us together,
what happened to everybody?" says Myrtle.
"We had scrapbooking,
they showed us how to make them so good."
She has framed the photographs with colored ribbons,
some names are in cut-out letters,
others in glitter, a few in fringe.

Every left-hand page in Annie's book has a sticker
of praying hands in the corner
with the page number in careful printing
and every right-hand page has a sticker of an angel.
The angels are of different kinds,

some adult, some babies, some flying,
some only hovering over the photos of the club friends.
"Look at her—Bonnie, she was real Godly,
now she quit school,
see what damage they did,
stopping the club?"

The names of the Jesus Club members come back to me
when I listen to the scrapbook stories.
Joe, who could stand on his head:
Myrtle has a photo of him doing it in her book.
And Beverly, with addicts for parents,
who was afraid of moving lights anywhere,
till she found safety in Jesus.

And Gary.
He still takes up four pages, six photos,
with angels holding golden cords
from the corners of them.
The floating angels have heavenly smiles,
or what I imagine might be heavenly smiles,
since I don't really have an iota of an idea.

## 27.

I am getting to the part I have been trying not to tell.
"I'll never forget
in my whole life how Gary sang on
'Peaceful as a River,'" says Myrtle, and she starts to sing:

> "Peaceful as a river,
> Jesus Love flows over and over
> I never knew such love so true
> there is peace within me now,
> within me now,
> within me now."

Annie sings with her, and starts to tear up in her eyes.
Myrtle and I put our arms around Annie.
"Did you ever hear more beautiful words
in your life?" Myrtle says, her head leaning to the side,
her eyes romantic.
"Stop! Stop it!" says Annie,
her body is tight and muttering,
and Myrtle and I don't know what to do
except keep our arms around her.

Gary.

He was there, he loved Annie.

And then he wasn't and he didn't.

But at least she got kissed.

## 28.

It happened at lunch.

With so much thinking about WIMS and the future,
I had not paid attention to right now,
and I only barely noticed
Annie had been putting hardly any food on her tray at all.
Some carrots and a little bit of soup and salad
and three cookies, and I thought it was all her desolation
over that boy
who wandered away with her heart,
she was barely beating without it.
And now, on top of that
she suddenly gets some kind of food poisoning
and pukes all over the cafeteria floor,
it even got in her hair.

Even if we went to a good school
food poisoning could be in the cafeteria.
If food is left out for all the long time it takes
to feed everybody in this big place.
Summer Science taught about *Clostridium perfringens*

and, too, there's a *Staphylococcus aureus*
that lurks in foods left too long at room temperature,
and I throw a dirty look toward the food counter
about their infected salad dressing
as I grab hold of Annie.

Myrtle is on one side, I'm on the other,
holding on to our parts of her,
trying to keep her hair back.
Naturally, it is not our first vomiting together.
Paper napkins flew to her side
and the sounds of an audience,
people turning around, pointing
from the tables nearby.
Poor Annie. It was a mess, of course.

Annie has had hard luck in her life,
and— Well, who hasn't? Who hasn't?
But still: those bad divorces,
her mom always trying so hard
and Annie never having a real bedroom of her own.
She was just fine after throwing up, though,
trying to forget it had happened.
I would, too. "The girl who threw up in the cafeteria"
is a terrible thing to be known as.

After the cafeteria mess
Annie went to her class in one hall
and Myrtle and I went running to ours in another.
I asked Myrtle if we should get hold of Gary
and tell him how bad she feels.
Myrtle rolled her eyes at me.
"Oh, he's hard to find, LaVaughn.
First he has a phone number, then he doesn't.
I don't know. I just wish Annie would get over him."

## 29.

Why did it take me so long
to comprehend about Annie?
She said she would not even bother going to school
for the rest of this week.
Myrtle coaxes: "Annie, school is school.
We go. Come on, you show up tomorrow."
"Why? What's the point?" says Annie.
We are at Myrtle's locker,
gathered to cheer Annie up.
Imagine not going to school.
Working in a horrible job with horrible hours,
ending up hopeless before you're old enough to vote.
We have seen it happen
more times than we could say.

"Annie, school *is* the point," I say,
but then I feel guilty for getting put in better classes.
I try to blink the guilt away.

"LaVaughn's right. For a change." Myrtle leans her body
into my right shoulder, sending a brief signal:
We are friends even after everything that happened.

I lean back into her.
"Come on, I'll let you wear my orange top,
I'll bring it tomorrow," says Myrtle.
I need something to offer. I say,
"I'll buy your lunch tomorrow. Come on, Annie."

Myrtle reaches into her locker, gets a bag of chips,
opens the bag and holds it out
level with my chin and Annie's nose.

Annie winces,
convulses, her throat spasms,
she throws up right there
in the hallway between us,
we barely have time to jump back.

Oh, no. Oh, no, no, no, no, no.
The world changed.
I hold out my jacket for shelter,
Myrtle is holding Annie's hair out of the way.
People bump into us as they try to walk by—
Around the edge of someone's backpack
Myrtle and I look at each other
just long enough for a heartbeat.
My mind windmills around
like crazed arms trying to wave off bats in the night,

whirling to try to drive away the facts,
which I'd do anything not to know.
I hold my jacket higher, straighter,
trying to make the truth not be true.

A thousand things Myrtle and I could say.
I started to say one of them, I'll never know which one.

In the air between Myrtle's face and mine
I saw bulging Annie,
growing a child inside,
we would be different forever.

## 30.

Annie wouldn't let us go home with her,
she even pushed us away as she got on the bus,
so we ran and got in the back door and stood.
We got out at her stop, we followed her,
she kept saying, "Go away. Go away. Go away."
We went all the way to her door,
which closed in our faces.

We stood on the sidewalk
of Annie's creepy block
which is only a little creepier than mine
and a little less creepy than Myrtle's.
I don't want to think about the microbial count
even just in front of the doorway.

I ask Myrtle, "What was the first thing you thought?"
Myrtle's shoulders go hard, her voice dangerous:
"I would tear that boy apart if I could find him."

I turn around and run two blocks
to get on a bus and go to WIMS.

## 31.

This memory comes back,
pushing its silly way onto the bus with me.

When we were little in school,
one of our teachers had a baby
and it was Annie who said
what we were all thinking:
"Eeeeewwwwww: What you have to do to get a baby.
I wouldn't never want to do that."
We tried to think about it and not think about it.
Myrtle said, "Well, if you're married a long time
and you knew him good enough,
then you could do it. If you knew him good by marriage."
And even saying that, her voice shifted,
afraid we would disagree.
And Annie said,
"If you wash his you know, his things
and his socks and everything
in with the towels and your clothes
you might know him good enough."

"I don't know," I said.

"Maybe there's some other way to get a baby."

"LaVaughn, that's crazy. You have to do it.
That's the only way," Annie said.
Myrtle agreed with her and I was outnumbered.

That was just a few years ago.

## 32.

Annie stays out of school for two days,
as if she were on an island far away.
I go to Myrtle's house after WIMS and laundry.
Her face is silently furious.

Myrtle's father has a job
doing janitorial in a medium-size office building at night,
he has kept it for three months
and we walk softly in her house in our socks,
not to wake him in the daytime,
not to break the spell.

We sit in their kitchen
listening to the little thp, thp, thp sounds
of her cat Peaches drinking.
This cat was extra in the world,
nobody wanted it,
and just by good luck Myrtle came along.
Now she's a contented, spayed, orangey-gold animal
sleeping in bed with Myrtle,
who believes God matched her up with Peaches.

"Myrtle, do you think
God wants Annie to have this baby?" I ask.
Myrtle thinks about it, not for the first time.

"Well, it's a precious life
and God loves every life," she says.

"But does God want Annie to have it so young,
all alone and have her whole life changed?" I ask her.
Peaches jumps up in her lap
and they cuddle,
the purring sound easing the air.

"I don't know," she says after a while.
Still not knowing,
we go to Annie's house after dark
in cold rain and fog.
She is huddled down on the couch,
which also folds out to be her bed,
with her Gospel Pals scrapbook in her lap.
Rain pours down outside.

It's Myrtle who says the words:
"Annie, what are you gonna do?"
I briefly dwell on how many thousands of years
girls have asked other girls this question.

Annie's eyes at first
go scared and then not.
"The Angels will be here," she says.

Oh. Angels. The angels on her scrapbook pages
are coming alive?
"How will they know where to be?"
I ask before I realize what a wrong question it is.
It is so wrong
that Annie doesn't bother to look at me.

"They'll know.
They're my Angels," she says,
her eyelids draping like curtains.
"LaVaughn, you just can't see them,
you aren't trying hard enough.
They even sing
at night when I can't go to sleep for worry.
I hear them.
You just don't try.
Does she, Myrtle?"

It's not easy in the middle, where Myrtle is.
Maybe she believes in angels,
but after their club went to rack and ruin

Myrtle is not so quick
to let things sweep her up anymore.

"LaVaughn, tell me you never saw a Angel," says Annie.
I tell her: "I have never seen an angel."
"Oh, LaVaughn, you are such a unbeliever,
you're probably driving them away
right now,
with your cold heart.
You're blind if you can't see Angels."

"What do they do?" Myrtle asks,
on her thin middle line
of not wanting to disbelieve entirely.

"They do what Jesus wants them to do," says Annie
and she is smiling a smile of secrecy.
"All things work together for good if you love God.
Romans 8:28," says Annie.

We don't get Annie to promise
to come to school the next day,
but she also is not so definite about quitting school
forever.

On our way to the bus Myrtle says her opinion
about angels:
"Number 1: If anybody needs angels
it's my dad
and look—do you see any angel
around my house? Do you hear any wings?
Not a chance."
This is true; Myrtle's dad is on and off drugs so often
it makes her mad and sad and everything else,
and her mom, too, plus disgusted.
Myrtle is extra certain to go to every class every day
because she is so determined
not to let herself be "down the drain with
discouragement,"
as she says.
I cheer for her all the time.


"Number 2: I figure no angel will help me,
nobody helped me yet.
Waiting for an angel would be real stupid.
Annie's completely right about Romans 8:28,
that's exactly what it says, all things work together for good
if you love God, but I sure wish Gary
would of never laid eyes on her.
He is definitely not an angel."

The bus comes, we find a seat.
We look at each other, joined in resentment of Gary.
"How did Annie get to be so trusting of him?" I ask.
I can't imagine such foolishness.

"Well, they got together at a meeting I didn't go to.
It was a meeting for—
Oh, LaVaughn, I don't want to tell you—"

"Tell," I tell her.

"It was a meeting about how to get rid of gays."
Myrtle bends her head away, not wanting to say this.

"Huh?" I ask. She is fidgety
but she's already started.
"Well, it was. Gary thought the club
could get rid of the gays
in government."

"Oh, Myrtle," I say.

"Well, they had a plan to start with gays in school.
Teachers, students. Get rid of them."

"Myrtle!" I say.

"Start with? Then what?"

"Well, then the ones that run the government,
I don't know, I didn't go to the—"

"The gays that run the government? Myrtle,
who's saying this? What kind of people—"

"Oh, some of the club,
I don't know, they said they had evidence,
gays are selling government secrets,
they're gonna make us all turn gay. . . ."
She tries not to look at me. I wait.
Finally, she looks up, sorrowful.
"That don't make sense, right?"

"No. It makes zero sense.
That's what Gary was up to?"

"Well, that and spreading God's word," Myrtle says,
looking away again.

"Wait a minute, Myrtle—"

"I gotta get off, see my stop coming?"

"Myrtle. Myrtle." My voice goes low, I lean close.
"Did Gary do those things to Jody's locker?
Write those words,
bash in the door?"

"LaVaughn, you don't want to know that,
I've gotta get off—"

I grab her arm,
almost tight enough to hurt.

"Not just Gary.
There was others," she says,
and in her face is our old friendship
sensible and true,
and I let her arm go
and she gets off the bus.

## 33.

Not four minutes went by
after I got in the door at home,
not four minutes.
Before my mom said,
"Well, Annie's got herself in a fix, hasn't she?"

How does she know so fast?
"How in the world do you know that?" I ask her.
She closes her eyes and shakes her head.
I don't know how moms learn to look like that.
"LaVaughn, it is not a hard thing to figure out,
I saw her near the bus stop,
she walked 3 steps, I could tell."

In order not to think about horrible Gary
I tell my mom what Summer Science taught us
about the end of three weeks of pregnancy
when the neural tube is formed, and from that comes
the whole central nervous system of the baby.
The cerebral hemispheres
and the brain stem and the spinal cord
all come from the formation of this tube.

But of course this makes me think about Gary anyway.

"Annie's way past 18 days," says my mom,
and I think about the cerebrospinal fluid
that cushions the baby's brain
and about the embryo's spinal cord getting formed.

"How much past?" I ask.
"Oh, she's probably three months, I think,"
says my mom. "About.
What's she gonna do?"

Wouldn't we all like to know?
"I don't know. I don't think she knows yet."
"She been to a doctor yet?" my mom asks.
I have not asked this
but I get on the phone with Myrtle
and we decide to gang up on Annie.
I'm assigned to call the clinic,
Myrtle is assigned to get Annie ready in her mind
to go there.

Of course all this distracts my attention
from every other thing, WIMS, classes,
my question mark life.
I still can't help trying to figure out if Annie's face shows

that she has done it with a boy.
Shows it in any way.
I know Annie's face from ear to ear
and I can't tell.
It's a mystery I have always wondered about.
Wouldn't a girl's face change,
and so would a boy's?
(But with terrible Gary, who knows?)
I keep remembering not to think about that
and go back to homework.

## 34.

Annie's mom?
She cried, she hung on Annie: "Don't be afraid,
don't be afraid, don't be afraid, don't be afraid,
don't be afraid,"
till Annie was more afraid than she had been.

My mom has her opinion ready:
"If that was you, LaVaughn,
I'd flay you." She is very clear:
both kidding and not kidding.
"Mom! You wouldn't flay me! You love me!"

"Love or not, no daughter of mine
will be bringing home a baby
when she's a mere child, and you don't forget that,
not ever, not ever. Yes, indeed, I would flay you."

But when I put my arms around her and say,
" 'Flay' is a terrible thing to do to somebody,"
she hugs me back and laughs in her throat,
very soft: "No, I would not flay you.
I'd beat you good, that's all."

This woman who never took anything harder than
a math paper to my backside.


It's Myrtle who takes charge:
she went to Annie's nutrition class the very next week,
and she began to manage Annie's diet.
Every day she lugs a cooler back and forth to school:
tangerines, dried apricots,
carrots, raisins, nuts, lettuce leaves, juices.
Myrtle's locker becomes a small cafeteria
of nourishment and good hopes for Annie.
And Annie can't go to Myrtle's house for the whole time
because being near cat feces
can cause brain damage to the fetus.


And Myrtle planned the pregnancy class attendance.
"Look, Annie. We'll go with you, we'll take turns.
Me and LaVaughn, your mom, your sister,
you won't have to be alone."
Annie watched Myrtle organizing her
from a little distance.
Myrtle went to Annie's mom and her sister,
got everybody's names on the right lines,
and within two days we knew our schedule,
which Myrtle had made copies of for our walls,
with little pictures of baby toys and teddy bears.

She tried getting some friends
from their church club of two years ago
but they didn't think they had time,
". . . with making a new club to get people saved,"
as their old friend from the Gospel Pals scrapbooks
told Myrtle.
Myrtle can get hissy
and she did. "You think that's Christian,
and helping Annie would not be Christian? Think again,"
she said, and she walked away. I have seen
Myrtle walk away. When you see her do it
you are not in doubt,
you know that girl is walking.
She phoned me, still steamed.

"We're gonna get Annie through this,
right, LaVaughn?"
And I feel greatly cheered
that for some mysterious reason
the three of us got put together in this bad neighborhood
with our little Head Start name tags and
our little jumping in mud puddles
on the way home from Head Start
and our little friendship
which has grown so big.

Myrtle assigned me the first pregnancy exercise classes,
to get Annie used to going.
We danced, we stretched, we bent, we reached,
and Annie wasn't so grumpy on the way home.
This girl who used to jump rope on the team:
now if we don't make sure she goes to the class
she sinks into grouchiness and sleepiness
and comes out murmuring to her angels,
in no words I can understand.

Myrtle brought her soda crackers and ginger capsules,
and the clinic gave her vitamin $B_6$ pills,
and her morning sickness is not so awful anymore.

"And folic acid! You've gotta take folic acid!"
Myrtle jabs a bottle of the pills into Annie's backpack.

Nobody mentions Holy Gary.
Myrtle tried five different phone numbers
and gave up.
At night I dream of babies gasping for breath.

## 35.

I have been in WIMS long enough
to fill three thick notebooks,
I have read chapters about illnesses
I would never have thought of:
things that can go wrong with the liver, an ear,
a collarbone.
In my group of "Never Right the First Time"
—Sophie, Naomi, Shar, Fanta, and LaVaughn—
we have been wrong and then right
about the femoral veins,
the external iliac veins, and others,
and we know them now. Subclavian veins: fun to say, too.
I have colored the digestive system
in our anatomy coloring book,
I can say lamina propria,
I have learned new things about spit.

Our schedule for the academic year is all calendared
in the front of our binder,
with Dr. Moore and Dr. Faleen taking turns teaching us.
Nerves, bones, organs, muscles, diseases of everything.
The lab skeleton wears a name badge: "Clear Claude."

I watch Dr. Moore watching our class:
"A firm understanding of science can be our backbone,
even when it seems we have none," she says,
waving to Clear Claude, our bony mascot.
Dr. Moore and Dr. Faleen are proud of us,
they have even started to like this lab joke.
Putting together our skeletons in the beginning was hard
but it helped us get to know one another, and
on the quiz I got osteosarcoma right,
and so did our whole team of five.
Such a horrible disease, primary bone cancer,
discovered in the early 1800s,
and it develops in the osteoid tissue,
sometimes in children.
"Every day there is a new loss,
every day we learn from that loss," says Dr. Faleen,
"and we reach the point where loss becomes insight.
It is much easier to learn this
as women studying medical science
than it is to learn it when we or our loved ones
are sick, injured, dying—
Much easier."

In these weeks we have learned a zillion new things:
For instance, when you soak your cut finger
in hydrogen peroxide every day

and then you wonder why it's not healing,
wonder no more: The solution kills bacteria *and* cells,
so it can't be healing your wound.
I know such things now.
I know Sophie's pulse and blood pressure
as well as I know my own,
we have listened with stethoscopes
to each other's heart, lungs, intestines
(Fanta's intestines sound funny, we all agree)
and now we could do it on anybody.
Even the way Dr. Moore says "neurotransmitters"
makes them sound like
things you'd want to be friends with.

We've taken quizzes and become more smiling.
Dr. Moore's smile is contagious, we discuss
in the bathroom.
Dr. Faleen puts it this way:
"The world we live in is full of danger and sadness,
and we have every reason to be afraid
of the next minute. The next second.
Terrible things can happen to all of us.
We are showing that we appreciate the gift of life
and are open to its pleasures,
however soon they may be cut off from us."

"We can better live with the weighted optimism
of our profession
if we smile," says Dr. Moore.
"And smiling changes blood flow patterns,
it actually lowers the temperature
of the brain's blood supply,
putting us in a better mood."

And today they surprise us.
"The new idea is this, girls:
You make us proud of you, we help you.
You show your serious intent,
we reward you. We pay you."

A little sound as Dr. Moore
shifts her papers on the lectern,
the gentle sound of her sleeve on paper.

"How do we pay you?
A very good question. Raise your hand if you have
a working computer in your home. Go ahead,
hands up."
The sound of people trying not to snort,
trying not to make sarcastic mouth motions
is all over this room. A computer?

Some of these students here
have never had a completely new jacket.
They study hard and they reserve school computers
early in the morning just like me,
they are here in this class
*in spite of* no computers in their houses.
We are not princesses with computers.
I am angry inside that this doctor
would make that assumption.

"I see. How would you like to have laptop computers?
Your very own?
To do your work?
To advance you toward your desired professions?"

From the second row I watch her eyes
scooping the room behind me, scooping me, too.
The body-shifting in chairs, legs uncrossing
reaching for solid ground,
breath poofing out from people's mouths.
Is she joking? Would a doctor be so mean?

"You may have figured out
that we are not kidding.
Forty-five laptop computers are waiting for homes.

And a grant to pay for whatever internet connections
you need.
Here's the sign-up sheet—"

Somebody gasps. Mostly we are gagged with surprise.

"Our department is getting new laptops.
You need the old ones.
Don't you?" Her voice, short and sure, rings.
Eyes bulge, some coughing happens.
I imagine my own keyboard,
my own screen. I can't imagine.

I turn around to look at the rows behind me.
These are faces in shock.
If our synapses were visible they would light up the room.
The students laugh, slap hands, make noise,
celebrating but doubting, too.

I look at Dr. Faleen. She is thrilled.
How excited you get when you give somebody something
you know they'll love.
Chocolate chip cookies go through my mind.
I push them away, as I always do.
I delete them.

I'm here in this room,
way more grown up than the child I was
those two years ago,
and this is an auditorium full of cheering people.

## 36.

My mom has stayed late, worked overtime for years,
all of it for me.
I have heard her on the phone to her friends,
". . . and LaVaughn she'll have to have a computer
*some*day.
She can't *not* have a computer,
not and do science like she wants,
I just don't know, I just don't know.
I just don't know."

What if it doesn't come true?
I squint my eyes shut and wait.

# 37.

But it does.
45 laptop computers
arranged on five carts
lined up in rows, they almost shine.
They could be in the Art Museum:
Look but don't touch.
We touch them.

"These are loaded for you," says Dr. Falleen.
"All you do is type in the code we've assigned you.
These are your academic bonus, girls.
Next week, the printers."

We leave the building,
45 girls with royal treasures in our backpacks,
we ride with the medical students down the hill,
and every one of us is smiling.

In my bedroom at home
I shout out the window
as if I were Jilly.
"Computer! Mine! Woo!"

And I stand in my own bedroom
centered in front of the keyboard
with the birds' nest in the tree on the ceiling
directly above it,
I hear the giggling sound of me
bouncing from wall to wall, silly with childish glee.

Within three days
the connections are done
and I am looking at the transparent zebrafish embryo
on my very own screen
with my mom standing behind me,
watching the fish develop from a single cell
to all its major organ systems,
and she goes speechless.

## 38.

Back in third grade
our teacher made us learn to write thank-you notes.

    Dear _____,
        Thank you for the _____.

And then we had to say one thing about the gift,
one sentence. Then we wrote "Yours truly" and our names.

It was so hard to think of that one thing to say.
We children who could chatter like squirrels
about anything
got so confused when we had to write one thing in thanks.
Myrtle's dad was in drug rehab
and her mom got her a new box of colored markers
to make her feel better,
and Myrtle made picture after picture with those markers
in orange, purple, green, pink, brown, red,
and yet she sat at her desk scowling
because the teacher said
we had to write that one thank-you
in a sentence.

We all mostly felt that way.
Writing the words of an important thing was so hard,
like a soap bubble you see clearly right in front of you
and then you reach for it and you break it.

Little Victor in our class wrote his thank-you note
with no trouble.

> Der Mumy,
>     Thank you for the mitens. There is 2 of
> them.
>     Yors truly
>     Victor

Not till after he was killed
so young, not till we thought back over his life
did we grasp what a hilarious thank-you note that was.
Little Victor, our classmate who died
before his voice changed.

Annie's mom would not let her go to Victor's funeral.
She thought Annie should not see tragedy so close,
but my mom and Myrtle's mom took us,
because "We will pay our respects to that poor woman
and to her little son,
we will not punish that poor woman

by not going to that child's funeral."

Over the years Victor has sometimes come back to me
in my thoughts, in my dreams,
he made the best original Lego men we ever saw,
and he marched them along the floor,
even the teacher was proud.
Victor and Jody were best friends
and Jody has to remember that every day of his life.

I have used that third-grade lesson
for every thank-you note I write.
To the Aunts for the watercolor paints when I was ten
and for all other gifts.
And I use it again
on the card to the doctors.

    Dear Dr. Moore, Dr. Faleen, and WIMS,
        Thank you very much for the computer.
    I have made room for it on my desk and I will
    use it for all my classes.
        Yours truly,
        LaVaughn

But this was not a letter I could send.

Dear Dr. Moore, Dr. Faleen, and WIMS,

I never thought I would have ~~such a thing as~~ a computer in my own home. When I walk in the door of my bedroom I ~~jump with surprise~~ am surprised. I ~~think I can~~ will do better in ~~all~~ my classes with this computer. ~~It has such things to discover, things that are amazing.~~ I found the zebrafish embryo and its nerve fibers first thing. I promise I will make ~~bigger~~ better progress now.

I am still so ~~astonished~~ surprised.

Yours truly,

LaVaughn


The part about the zebrafish embryo was too silly.


Dear Dr. Moore, Dr. Faleen, and WIMS,

When I looked up the zebrafish embryo on my new computer I was surprised how easy it was. ~~I have never had a computer~~ I never imagined a computer being in my very own room on my very own desk. And now this computer will ~~get me to be~~ make me a better student.

Yours truly,

LaVaughn

That was too dull.

Dear Dr. Moore, Dr. Faleen, and WIMS,
I am amazed! I am so surprised when I
wake up in the morning and see a computer in
my own room! It is so wonderful! Thank you!
Yours truly,
LaVaughn

That was too short and it sounded childish.

Dear Dr. Moore, Dr. Faleen, and WIMS,
The new laptop will make ~~a~~ the difference
in my ~~life~~ school life. ~~I am so excited about it~~
~~I shouted out my window down to the alley.~~ I
will be a better student being able to look up
~~anything~~ many of the things I need to know.
Thank you from the bottom of my heart.
Yours truly,
LaVaughn

This too was a wrong letter
but I licked it shut and sent it anyway.

In the night I woke, turned on the computer,
looked up the Art Museum,

rambled through the rooms
till I came to the bronze lovers
and stared at them,
how shiny their curves and muscles are,
how they stare face to face.

If I could love a machine
I'll grow to love this one,
this mine, this reservoir, this cave of treasure,
this quiet hump of education and answers
and more questions
in my very own bedroom,
this friend.

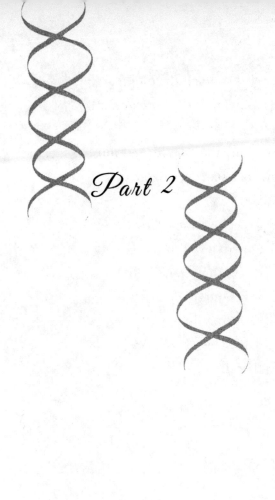

Part 2

## 39.

It started as a whisper in the WIMS bathroom
with a toilet flushing:
"*Whshshshwshwshshshs* baby died."
"No! Really?"
"Yeah, the *whshshshshwhshhshhh*
and it *wshshshshwhshshsh*."
"Poor *thing*."
"That's why she *wshshshshwhshshsh*."
"Really?" "Really." "No!" "Really!"

Whose baby? How did it die?
Is the "she" one of us?
Somebody's tragedy is walking around with us?
And what if she's sitting next to me
and I say something clunky
and make her feel worse?
And Annie!
Annie!

## 40.

I kept listening, I followed those girls,
pretending to look for a pen in my bag,
bending to scratch my ankle,
I hovered.

And I heard more. Not much.
Hanging up our lab coats
the next day:
"She just can't help helping girls.
It's in memory of that dead child."

"Even the laptops.
She didn't have to give them to us."
"I heard she does this every year. Imagine
making your baby's death into a gift
for other people. It makes me cry."

Dr. Moore.
Naturally, I looked at her with new sight.
I imagine my mom losing me
when I was a baby
and my stomach goes turbulent—

How she would suffer.
She would have had some other baby sometime
but she would always wonder about me,
how my legs, my arms would feel,
what my voice would have been.

Dr. Moore: going through her life
mourning and grieving.
I watch her, sometimes in her thick glasses
and sometimes wearing contact lenses,
blinking at us all.
Would I do that? Could I stand there, pacing, eager,
pointing with my hands,
emphasizing,
smiling such a contagious smile,
teaching us more than we can learn all at once?

No, I could not.
I sit in the class
and my heart goes straight from my seat
in the second row
to this courageous doctor,
and as she is talking about the amazing things
medicine can do,
she says, "But every step forward
brings with it concomitant dangers.

For instance, human patients
who have animal organ transplants
may contract xenozoonosis,
any of several diseases caused by microorganisms
that may bypass the normal defenses of the recipient.
Microorganisms are the most adaptive things
we know of, remember that.
What is non-pathogenic in its natural host
may become pathogenic in a human being.
Any questions?"

Two girls ask about pig organ transplants,
and Dr. Moore answers them, smiling,
naming two books and a website
without checking her notes,
and my heart cringes for her
and her lost child.

## 41.

Every Tuesday and Wednesday
I ride the bus up the hill past the cemetery,
memorizing pathophysiology data.

I have wondered for quite a long time
whether or not life is one big tragedy.
Sometimes it seems to be
and sometimes not.

Where is Dr. Moore's baby buried?
What would you do with the body of your dead baby?
What in the world would you do?
And Annie? If her baby died?
Lately, everything makes me think about her.

We had Women Scientists Day
and we all got to research one,
wear a costume, be that person,
and tell the whole class about her in two minutes.
I had already been Gregor Mendel (1822–1884)
in Summer Science,

and now I got to choose my own woman scientist.
"Most of these names will not be familiar to you yet,"
said Dr. Faleen. We were to go to a costume shop
and tell them we were from the WIMS class
and get costumes for free.
"They are friendly to us," Dr. Moore told us,
"they understand our important work."


Fanta on my lab team found Aglaonike
from ancient Greece
who could predict eclipses of the moon,
when and where they would happen.
She might have been the first woman astronomer
but she knew so much that people suspected her,
thought she was a sorceress
because when she said the moon was going to vanish
it vanished.


Sophie was Virginia Apgar (1909–1974),
one of the first women doctors to specialize in childbirth.
"Dr. Apgar invented the Newborn Scoring System,
it's called the Apgar score," Sophie told the class.
She was wearing clunky shoes and a dress of the 1940s
and old-fashioned glasses and a stethoscope.
"You examine the baby one minute after birth

and then five minutes later.
For appearance, reflex response, pulse, muscle tone,
and respiration.
The scale runs from zero to 2 on each of those,
and a total 8 to 10 means the baby is healthy.
She wanted to be a surgeon,
but doctors said she shouldn't because she was a woman.
And she was the very first person
to find a way to evaluate the health of a newborn.
And here are the score sheets." She hands them out,
everyone gets a page showing how to score a newborn.

Shar picked Madame Marie Sklodowska Curie
(1867–1934)
who discovered two new elements, polonium and radium,
invented the word "radioactivity,"
won a Nobel Prize with her husband
and another one by herself.
"What did she think of her life when she was dying
of radiation poisoning from her own lab work?"
is the way Shar ended her two minutes.
We all knew too much about cells to answer.

Naomi was Rosalind Franklin (1920–1958).
"Back then, only these few scientists

were even thinking about DNA shape,
and Franklin designed a tilting microfocus camera
and she kept bubbling hydrogen gas
through salt solutions in the camera
and taking X-ray diffraction photographs.
After 100 hours of doing this, her photograph number 51
showed the double helix shape of DNA,
and the secret was out.
She died of cancer
before the two scientists who won the Nobel Prize
used her photograph 51
and didn't say her name with it.
So I won't say their names today,
but here's photograph 51,"
and we each got a copy
of the microscopic X pattern, the double helix
that changed science forever.
"I made the copies from my WIMS laptop
and I printed them on my WIMS printer.
Thanks, WIMS!" said Naomi,
and she plunked down into her chair,
a relieved girl with her speech over.


I wrote things down about all 44 women scientists,
and I got to be the ancient Si Ling Chi.

This Empress of China in 2640 BCE
sat in her royal garden watching silkworms
and noticed how they were spinning their thread.
She invented the process
of taking the thread out of the cocoon,
she set up silk cultivation farms
more than 5,000 years ago. Think of it:
Sitting in your own royal garden, saying to yourself,
"Those worms are weaving something.
We could use that."
Thousands of other people
had passed through the very same garden,
not bothering to notice.
"Noticing. That's what Si Ling Chi did,"
I said at the end of my two minutes,
and I said "Thank you" in Mandarin Chinese,
"Shyeh shyeh," which isn't hard to learn.

Afterward Dr. M. says we should all go to the cafeteria
and have tea. "As many of you as can,
please join me in the south end," she invites.

Only a dozen of us don't have to be somewhere else
right away,
and Dr. Faleen has to jump out of class every time

to dash home to her children
("jump and dash," she calls it),
so the small group of us, including Sophie and me,
carry our costumes in their crinkly bags
down to the basement cafeteria,
and we all get tea at the counter,
which is not a beverage I know much about how to drink.
I don't know how to choose a flavor.
I get the kind Dr. Moore gets.
The paper cup is hot and I try to balance it
with everything else I am carrying.
When I get to the south end
I see Dr. Moore has brought a whole big tin of cookies,
home-baked.
"Oh, oatmeal cookies are good for you,"
she laughs and passes the tin around.
"I knew you'd work hard today,
so I baked these last night. . . ."
We each take one, and I can see others are nervous too
at this surprise.
I am embarrassed to be in this accidental group,
an ancient Chinese empress
who doesn't know how to drink tea
(do you put sugar in it? or what?)
with this famous doctor and her generous heart,

teaching us medicine and history and baking treats for us.

She brings up organ transplants again and tells us
this very hospital has two specialists who do them
several times a week.
"You know, we're just at the beginning,
so many things we don't know yet. . . ."

We are eating cookies, drinking tea,
smiling around the table
with the woman who invented WIMS for us,
and this section of the world seems to be ours,
free of charge.
Under the table, our legs sprawl as if they could lift off.

Sophie from my lab team says,
"Dr. Moore, when I get really afraid on a test
I crumble up inside,
I can't remember a protein chain or anything,
what should I do?"
I lean forward and others do, too,
so we can hear every word from Dr. Moore
on this crucial topic that every one of us knows
like a dark tunnel.

Dr. Moore looks straight ahead into the air, and says,
"Well, you'll just have to study harder
so you don't crumble up inside, that's all."
She sips her tea.

Sophie flinches just the teeniest bit
and says, "OK, I'll do that."
I feel eleven other pairs of legs shift under the table,
and I am not imagining things.

Sophie doesn't speak again
in the whole half hour that we stay there with our tea.
Others fill in the empty space
with pancreas questions, bone questions,
blood-brain barrier questions.
Dr. Moore answers them from her memory,
opening the right file in her brain for each fact
each time.

Sophie was the first one of our team to figure out
where the cervical vertebrae stop
and the thoracic ones begin
and she can point out the subclavian veins every time.
She did a whole report on microbicides.
She has four little brothers and sisters

and has to babysit them
till her mom comes home from work near midnight.
I think everybody could use some encouragement
about how not to crumble up inside
and she did not get it. I try to send her helpful thoughts,
pointing them out the side of my head toward hers.

I go to the bathroom to think,
hoping to understand it better in there,
which doesn't happen.

I'm the last out of the bathroom
and Dr. Moore is just putting the lid on the cookie tin,
we end up just us two waiting for the elevator.

Instead of running back to the bathroom
in hope that it will all get clear,
I stand in place
wishing to be someone else for the moment,
to be Si Ling Chi, staring at silkworms.
We get into the elevator, headed up from the basement.
I look at the wall
as Dr. Moore stared at the air when she answered Sophie.
But the instant the door closes,
Dr. Moore says, with her smile,

"You've got the gleam, LaVaughn."

Of all the things I could say to this announcement,
I hear myself answer, "What?"
She goes right on: "I mean, it's there: earnestness.
The passion to learn
and make meaning from life. It's a gleam."
She laughs.
"And you have it, girl. Don't you dare lose it.
'Bye. See you next Tuesday."
Then she is out of the elevator
and I continue on up to the sky bridge
where I cross and go to the bus stop.

The gleam.
I have it.
The air pings with astonishment.

Doesn't Dr. Moore know
how many times I have crumbled up inside?
If she saw me when I'm crumbling up
she would snatch my gleam away on the spot.

On the bus are the people in lab coats short and long,
high-spirited, laughing through their tiredness.

I wonder if they ever crumble up inside,
I want to tug on their sleeves and ask.
I sit in my seat and watch the cemetery go past.

How can you know if somebody has the gleam?
If you were smart enough, could you tell by looking?

## 42.

My gleam is private, not for telling,
but I made a Guidance appointment the very next day.

When it's my turn with the Guidance Man
I march through the door
and shake his hand like a genuine grownup
and he calls me LaVaughn
and I tell him I want to go to City University.

He steps back and looks at me:
"Well, LaVaughn, we are here to help you
with the next steps.
Do you know two adult professionals
who will write letters of recommendation for you?
A university reads those letters very carefully,
a letter can make them notice you."
He sees me looking vague.
"These letters must say you're of good character,
motivated and serious about your work."
"Huh?" I say. "Of good what?"
He sees I am blank, an empty jar.

His face gets disappointed,
as it did long ago when I didn't know how to shake hands.
"Oh, LaVaughn. You don't know?"
I shake my head laterally,
a word I know but he hasn't asked me for.
"Well, people have thought for thousands of years
about what character is. I suppose it's"
—he glances out his grimy window
with the two sets of bars across it—
"well, it's that you know the difference
between right and wrong,
and you act in accordance with your conscience,
using that insight."
He nods, agreeing with what he has just said.

"Oh," I say. So many wrong things I have done,
and things I didn't do right enough.
I could count hundreds of small ones of both kinds,
including being mean to Patrick long ago,
and others I have probably hidden back in history.

"Two adult professionals." He waits.
Dr. Rose's face comes into my mind, lifesize,
saying, "LaVaughn, an orderly mind can be
your best friend.

It will let new friends in
and can keep enemies out."
"There's Dr. Rose, I think?"

"Is that a question, LaVaughn?" asks the Guidance Man.
"Don't you *know*?"
I hunker down between my shoulders. Clavicles.
"LaVaughn, let me remind you:
My job is that of a conveyor belt.
I'm supposed to move you along,
keep you going in your education.
That does not include answering questions
you yourself already know the answers to.
Now: Is there Dr. Rose or not?"
He looks strict
as if I had not done a good job on handshaking
three minutes ago.

"Yes. There's Dr. Rose," I say.
"Good. That's one. Now, another one?"
Dr. Moore and her "weighted optimism" come up next.
I make an instant promise to myself
never to let her see me crumble up inside,
not even one blink of a crumble.
"Well, there's Dr. Moore
at the Women in Medical Science class

on Tuesdays and Wednesdays," I say.
The Guidance Man remembers.
"Oh, yes, you got into that group.
Congratulations, LaVaughn.
We're proud of you. Has Dr. Moore noticed you?"

"Yes," I say. I keep quiet about my gleam.

So we are decided, the Guidance Man and I,
and I take the papers and thank him and he smiles
at my handshake.
"Even when you don't want to, LaVaughn," he says.
"Don't want to what?" I use manners in my voice.

"Knowing the difference between right and wrong,
you act according to your conscience,
even when you don't want to. Character."
I take this in from his dependable face,
I shake his hand again, and I go on my way.

Before my gleam disappears
I ask Dr. Moore
to write the letter,
I give her the papers the Guidance Man gave me,
I make sure I have them all in order.

She has the letter done by the next day.
The very next day.
*That* is an orderly mind.
She tells me she has sent it to the Guidance Office
at my school
and she thanks me.
"Thank you for thinking of me in this capacity,
LaVaughn.
We believe in your future."

Even Dr. Rose took a week.
She said she was glad to see me
during a noisy lunch break
when we were smushed together in Hallway B.
"LaVaughn, the fact that I am proud of your progress
should have little or no effect on your progress,"
she says, smiling her smile that she would not let us see
till we had spent months with her after school
learning how to be more incisive thinkers,
as she would say.

"Of course I'll write a letter of recommendation,
of course I will. I expect you to rise to the occasion . . ."
" . . . which is life," I say back to her. Suddenly I wish
for those good old days in her class.

Catching her this way,
during lunch break,
I just want to go back, not forward.
Back to when she said, in that voice like a tower,
"ambivalent. To feel two ways about the same thing.
'Ambi-' from the Greek, meaning 'both.'
'Valent,' from the Latin, meaning 'going.'
Remember: Feeling ambivalent
is a crucial step in the process of living thoughtfully.
When we notice our ambivalence and examine it,
*then* our minds can thrive."

Jostled by shoulders and elbows from all sides,
she looks at the papers from the Guidance Man.
"Life is hard, LaVaughn.
I can't begin to describe how hard.
I will write this letter for you. It will be my pleasure."
In this pushed-together crowd of chatter and shouts,
I thank her and shove my way
through the congested hall,
to go on going forward.

## 43.

And then suddenly in the WIMS bathroom:
"Yes, her baby did too die."
"No. That baby's alive."
"How do you know? How could you know?"
"Somebody said."
"What kind of somebody?"
"Somebody that didn't get into WIMS."

"See? What do they know?"
*Whshshshwhshshshwhshshsh*, a toilet flushed,
then another one.
"It doesn't make sense that that baby didn't die."
"Well, it doesn't make sense that he did."
"And she's a *doctor*."
*Whshshshwhshshsh.*

It's way too tangled
to figure out.
Some gossip is true, other gossip is not,
it must be the way of the world.
Something new to baffle you every day of your life.

## 44.

"Weighted optimism" is on my mind
as WIMS students walk into the lecture hall.
Does it mean you hope for the best
but you know life is a tragedy
so that weighs your hope down from flying up on a whim?
I keep thinking about Annie.

Sophie comes in, sits next to me.
"See what I found last night," she says,
and shows me her book open to a page about potassium
with a picture of bananas
and a section about stomach jitters.
Bananas are loaded with potassium
which we need for cellular function,
nerve impulses, muscle action, and heartbeat.
The fructose energizes us,
and, because bananas have B vitamins,
they help neurons produce serotonin,
which is a neurotransmitter
and we all know how Dr. Moore loves neurotransmitters.

Sophie and I look at each other and say: "Bananas."
I read somewhere that the smart person
is the one who can build a lifeboat.
I whisper this to Sophie and she elbows me in thanks.

I take a moment to pretend I'm up on the ceiling
looking down at all of us.
The human brain weighs about 3 pounds, times 45 girls,
making about 135 pounds of brains
in these comfy chairs,
all getting encouraged on two afternoons each week.
And my mind shifts from Annie to Jolly,
whom I haven't seen in days.

Most of her luck is bad,
maybe getting born was the exception.
I suppose it's just luck she didn't end up
a baby in a Dumpster.
She never had folks except that one foster grandmother,
that long time ago, the one who said
Jolly should come back and visit her
and then died.

And Jolly remembers a nun was nice to her once
in a bus station.
And then she lived in a refrigerator box

and people bullied her.
Her good memories she can count
on the fingers of one hand.

What else can I guess?
I don't want to.
I don't want to imagine the people
who were terrible to her.
Hit her, ignored her,
got her pregnant
and then disappeared.

She is in my mind this Tuesday afternoon
while I wait with my new friends and my privileges,
Jolly: her messy, uneasy worrying,
her grouchy impatience,
the way she throws down her books and groceries
on the counter and rolls her eyes at the world.

It's one minute till lecture time.
I open my notebook to the new page.
Dr. Moore comes in,
rushing to the lectern,
she throws her books down on the desk beside it,
they land with a whackish thump
and shift among themselves,

she rolls her eyes
and lets her breath out in a whoosh—

LIKE THAT!
*That* is what I meant. About Jolly.
How she thumps things down and rolls her eyes
and breathes out in a whoosh.
That's what I meant. That kind of whoosh.

Then Dr. Moore smiles
her illuminating smile that we all expect to see.
(Is this a smile that her baby did not die after all?
Or a smile in spite of her tragedy?)
I pull my pen up out of my pocket
and get ready to take notes,
which I don't know very well how to do,
and I keep thinking the other girls
sitting in all these 44 other chairs
must know more about it than I do.
I write "systemic capillaries" and "oximeter"
and keep listening.

## 45.

And then Dr. Moore moved her arm.
Just lifted it and did something with her hair,
a gesture,
her right arm supinated,
the brachialis and biceps brachii moving,
the radius and ulna rising and falling,
just a reflex. Something knocked together in my mind
so fast I barely noticed,
I only felt my pen lift up off the paper
and settle back down.
Something so peculiar,
something so familiar,
I didn't track it
and went on listening about the thinness of capillary walls,
how blood cells can pass through them in single file.

Underneath, my subconscious was at work
connecting things
without my help,
going on pursuing a thing
that was not even a question yet,
when I thought I had forgotten it.

Till breakfast the next day.
In my orange juice
there was a feeling of little Jeremy,
I thought it was how he likes oranges, always has.
No, it was more than that.
Some linking thing,
some reaching thing wanting to touch something else.
Jeremy in my orange juice.
I didn't get it.

Two hours later
another jostling came into my mind
when I caught the spiral of my math notebook
on my sweater. Something about Jolly,
what she would say at such a time. Blaming the notebook,
blaming the sweater.
It too went away.

Not till WIMS class did it come out again,
some recognition
from my under-brain
into the light of day
and it stuck around,
and I began to ask a question I had never asked before.

## 46.

"What do you mean, you have to know?"
Jolly is testy with me
because I am asking her about her past life.
We're in the park with Jeremy and Jilly, it's a sunny day
and just to watch their little legs running
improves the weather.

"Jolly, I *like* you." Her eyes get funny,
something in them pulls back,
like sneaking out of the room.
"I mean, don't you think it would be *good*
to tell somebody?
About when you were little?"

She looks up, she looks down,
she looks over to where Jeremy is climbing
on a metal horse with springs under it.
Jolly has told me
only little bits about her life.
Now she makes her face go blank
and looks past my shoulder
to the stone wall at the edge of the park.

"I was a state award.
Award of the state,
there was a lot of us.
I had a red purse in 6th grade
from a big box of things we could choose,
I got that purse, then somebody stole it.
It had 2 parts, 2 places you could put things.
They wouldn't let us go in the bathroom at night,
we had terrible cereal in the morning.
That was in Residential. You have to go to Residential
when you're big."

I fumble for the right questions to ask.
"Well, you told me about the Gram,
your foster Gram?"
"Yeah, one of my foster ones, my foster Gram,
she did me nicer than anybody. You know what?"

"What?" I say, trying not to have any tone of voice at all
because that's what upsets Jolly: a tone of voice.
"She let me color in books on the table."

I listen to this small kindness somebody did.
"She must have been—"

"They made me go in the low group,

I didn't know my colors,
the teacher said you don't know your colors
you go in the low group.
And my foster Gram
she got me all new crayons, my own box.
She did the coloring books with me
we did them on the table,
she wouldn't let none of the other kids color on my books.
The teacher put me at the other group,
I knew my colors."

Jilly brings her three twigs to hold.
Jolly stares at them in her hand.
"And you know what else?
She made me a birthday cake,
she baked it in the stove all by herself.
Chocolate, with frosting too,
and candles,
I got to blow them out, everybody clapped."

"How many candles were there, Jolly?"
"Nine. There was nobody better than her,
till she died."
"Who was 'everybody'—when everybody clapped?"

"Her fosters, the kids and the grownup ones.

They all was there. That Jeremy I told you about,
him too.
She sewed my name on her shirt,
with all the others, she fed us good,
I even had nice pajamas,
she knit me a little sweater.
A green one. She made one for all of us.
Different colors.
I never knew anybody like her."
Her voice has more vitamins
than I've heard from her in so long,
telling these secret happy facts.

She looks up at the blue, blue sky
and her voice deflates again.
"They said we worked her to death, she died."
And Jolly's face goes the way I have seen it
so many times,
as if she has turned down the heat inside herself.

"Jolly!" I say, and I could have stopped myself
but I didn't.
"You didn't work her to death.
She just died. It wasn't your fault."

The corner of her mouth frowns down

as I have seen it many times before,
"They said we did, a counselor and a aide,
they said we killed her."

"Oh, Jolly! They lied to you!"
She goes to help Jilly get on a swing,
and she pushes her. Jilly goes back and forth
in a swooshing arc, grinning,
her mind on swinging.

I walk over to Jeremy's sproinging horse
and I'm the cowboy riding next to him,
we lasso some cows
the way we read about in a book.
We round up 98 cows
according to Jeremy.

Next, Jeremy climbs on the bars,
reaching and rising from bar to bar,
the dearest boy I ever knew.
I hush down my voice to say in Jolly's ear,
"Jolly, you did not kill your foster Gram."

"Shut *up*, LaVaughn."
This is Jolly's loud verdict.
She knows she shouldn't talk like that

in front of the kids
but she does it anyway
to make me stop.

That's all I get from her this time.
But I'm not finished.
Jolly was a ward of the state.
I never knew that before.
I begin to get it about her hairbrush.

Next day I watch Annie
feeding on Myrtle's Pregnancy Diet,
which Myrtle checks all the time:
"Annie, you got those raisins in your pocket?
Annie, you gotta have this salad,
I'm gonna watch you eat 3 bites.
Here, take these fig bars for 6th period,
you know how you're gonna feel by then."

Myrtle is so watchful, she's the one behaving like a mom.

Mothers and babies.
Did somebody steal Dr. Moore's baby? Kidnapped?
Too horrifying to think about.

*47.*

It's another good day,
Jolly has already passed one of her G.E.D. tests
and she has not quit any of her classes
this whole term.
I ask her about school when she was little.

As usual, she squinches up her face
in resentment that I'm asking. Then she starts:

"Well, they had the Learning Center place,
I had good teachers there, they sat with you,
they didn't just leave you alone by yourself,
and I knew my colors from Gram.
They had books with pictures.
They had snacks,
they had counselors for you to talk to,
they even remembered my name, most of them.
One of them said she'd take a bunch of us to a movie
but she got fired so we didn't.
But the government cut it off,
they cut off the whole place, closed it down.

"So there wasn't that place no more.
LaVaughn, I don't want to do this anymore today.
I got two little kids to look after,
don't you even *know* that?"

This isn't getting to what I really want to know,
but it's progress.
How did she get the name Jolly?

The next morning
Patrick crosses my mind
as I pass the closed science lab doors at school,
and my mind forgets to turn left in the next hallway,
making me miss three minutes of math.
It's because he told me the nuns took him back
when a foster family didn't work out.

It doesn't sound as if anybody ever took Jolly back.
I can't stop asking her questions, I have to keep on.
Why does bad luck follow her around?

## 48.

Jolly has been telling me these small bits,
then her eyes go scared, she tells me I'm dumb to ask
and just to shut up about it. Then she starts to tell.

It's a gray Saturday, we are all in the playground
where squirrels scutter and children shout.
"At the picnic they had a climbing thing
like that one over there,
the ladders and platforms was the same like these here,
you could get a handhold and swing yourself up,
it was like being in the sky." Jolly's voice sounds easy,
as if the roof will not fall in on her today.
I ask, "What picnic was that?"

"Oh, they had adopting picnics.
They take you all in a van,
you get to play on the swings and things.
You go there looking as cute as you can,
the Residential counselors make sure your socks
are straight,
they tell you don't fall down & get yourself dirty.

"People come & look over you,
about if they want to adopt you,
you wear a name tag.
Sometimes they say, 'What is your name.'
You tell them 'Jolly' and they go, 'Oh, that's a *nice* name!'
One lady asked me did I like pink
for a bedroom set. I said 'Yeah I do.'
I didn't know what a bedroom set was
but I thought it was the right answer.
And she said did I like to see movies
and I told her Yeah then too.
She put her hands on my shoulders,
both hands,
and she said, 'Are you a good girl?'
and I said Yeah again.
Then she said, 'Well. Well.'
And I never saw her again."

This lurching life Jolly has had,
tightening her face
and going along and going along—
I don't think I could do it from one day to the next.
I don't think I could.

"Services gives you a hot dog and ice cream.

And Oreos."

"Services?" I ask.
"*Chil*dren Services, LaVaaaawwwwnnnn.
Children *Services*.
The people that have the picnic.
*They* give you it.
Don't you know *any*thing?" Jolly's eyes ridicule me.
No, I do not know anything.
Not compared with the story of Jolly's life.

"Oh, I dreamt about that," she gentles down,
"I dreamt it a lot,
that pink bedroom set
I dreamt it was a pink bed
with pink blankets
and a pink thing beside the bed
where you put your other clothes, it would have drawers,
pink ones with knobs and they worked.
I dreamt that lady
and her hands on my shoulders."

Jolly stops talking and looks up
to where Jilly is singing on top of the play structure:

*"Mewwy had a little lamb,*
*little lamb, little lamb,*
*little lamb, little lamb,*
*little lamb, little lamb,*
*little lamb, little lamb. . . ."*
Jilly's voice chirps out over the park.

"There was ruffles."
I look at Jolly blankly, my mind on Jilly's song.
"The bedroom set," she says,
looking away
to Jeremy, who is drawing pictures in the dirt with a stick.

"Always hot dogs and Oreos and ice cream.
You get all smiley for the adopting families,
you go with high hopes,
you keep trying to look nice,
you always behave good.

"Some kids get picked,
mostly kids don't get picked.
You go back to Residential
and it's plain as a day nobody wants you.
They put away your good clothes for the next time.

"The last adopting picnic

I left.
I walked out of the park. I didn't know I would
but I had $15 and I just walked.
They give me money for looking after the little ones,
$15 was the most ever.

"I was a case load,
they didn't even call me my name half the time,
I was tired of being a case load.

"I was sprised it was so easy.
Shocked is more like it.
I just took off my name tag and it went in the trash.
I walked to where some kids hung out in the underpass
way far from here,
that's where the Box Boys & Box Girls was living,
they said Come on stay,
they had a extra box,
so I stayed. It was so easy
I was sprised."

"But when they came looking for you, Jolly?
They must've—"

"Looking for me? Maybe. I don't know.
Kids was always coming and going at Residential,

counselors, too.
People got fired,
new kids come from abuse or emergencies,
and from being extra someplace,
people got moved around,
especially the big ones,
you'd get to know somebody and they'd disappear.
Some kids went to Protection,
that was if they had bruises showing
or sores. Some went cuckoo.
You'd wake up in the morning
and somebody went cuckoo in the night
while you was asleep.

"I didn't know I was gonna disappear that day.
I just did it. It wasn't a plan.
I had the $15 so I walked."

And so she made herself a random girl.
I decide to take a chance and push for more.
"How did you explain, Jolly?
I mean when people asked you,
when you—when you just turned up like that.
How did you explain?"

Her eyes take their time deciding to tell me.
"I made up that mom.
I made pretend.
That mom with the pink bedroom set,
I guess they believed me.
She was way too busy to worry about me
so I run away.
It wasn't hard to make up."

As we leave the playground
Jeremy asks,
"LaVaughn, how come beetles gots 2 sets of wings
and flies only gots 2 wings total?"
He is clutching his insect book
that I have told him and told him not to try to read
when we're crossing streets.

"I don't know. That's the way it is.
They evolved that way."
Jolly picks Jilly up so we can walk faster.

"Is that all they need, just 2 wings?
Flies?" Jeremy keeps on asking.

"I don't know. Why would they only need two

if the beetles—" I grab his hand and we all begin to run
toward the bus stop—
"Here, let me carry the book." I grab it.

Jeremy keeps on. "I mean
if they're only gonna live just a teensy time,
maybe they won't need all those wings,"
and he's puffing, running along. "That's why. Huh."

We get on the bus, Jolly sits Jilly down
and we get arranged.

"Most of the Box Kids was high,"
Jolly whispers to me. "Most of the time."
I go from insect wings back to the underpass
where Jolly lived in a box.
"Smokin' things, swallowin' things,"
she whispers, still catching her breath.
"You like them drugs,
drugs end up hating you,
I learned that much."

Jilly points at a fire engine out the bus window
and we all converse and admire it.

I go home

with much too much to think about,
my neurons busy and jumpy,
my brain pressing on my skull.
I look up at the birds in my private painted bedroom tree
and close my eyes.

## 49.

The very next day
Jolly has a note from Jeremy's kindergarten,
they want her for a conference,
and she gets after him: "Jeremy, what did you do?
You gotta have behavior in kidneygarden,
that's your job. Now what's gonna happen to us?"
Jeremy looks up at her
and goes back to the book he is reading
about frogs and tadpoles,
which he wants, live ones.
But she goes to the conference
and Ricky goes with her
and I sit the kids.

Before bedtime we measure each other
on the measuring wall that Ricky made.
You stand in your sock feet against the doorframe
and somebody holds a ruler flat on your head,
trying to keep the ruler parallel with the floor.
These are Jeremy's instructions,
"parallel wid da floor down dere,
so you can do measurin'."

Then you step carefully out from under the ruler
and look at how tall you are, compared with last time.
The ruler person continues to hold it still
and somebody else goes in under the ruler
to make a dark pencil line on the door frame.
This is your height
and we write your name beside that line
and the new date.
Jilly is nearly two centimeters taller
than last time I measured her.
And her pajamas are getting tight.
I remind myself to look in the Goodwill next week.

Jilly walks toward her mother's hairbrush,
watching me watching her
and I surprise myself: "Jilly, do *not* touch your mother's
*own private personal hairbrush,* do you *hear* me?"
Jilly doesn't recognize this new, hard voice
that comprehends why Jolly protects her hairbrush.
I pick her up and hold her close,
this girl with her complicated history.

I get them organized into bed, books and all,
I get my broken treaties of history homework
spread out on the table
and I hear them discussing, as usual, in the dark.

Jeremy is telling a story.
"So the four Billy Goat Gruffs went over the bridge. . . ."
"No! Thwee. Thwee Billy Goat Gwuffs. It was thwee."
"You just hold still and listen.
The four Billy Goat Gruffs went over the bridge. . . ."

"I'm telling LaVaughn on you—"

And now Jeremy gets his exasperated voice:
"I'm making you up a new one
and you won't even let me.
So the four Billy Goat Gruffs went over the bridge
and on the other side was two turtles—"

"Theoh was no two tuhtles oveh theoh!"

"LaVaughn! Jilly won't let me tell her no story!"

I go in there and I say,
"Listen, Jilly, lots of little girls in the world
never even heard one story,
they never even heard of any Billy Goats Gruff at all.
And you've got Jeremy telling you extra ones
and you don't want them? Jilly, think about it.
You're getting special goats.
Here, we'll both listen."

She scoots for me,
I lie down next to her, scooting *Goodnight Moon* away,
she cuddles her head against my neck
breathing warm on my skin,
she whispers, "Good night woom,
good night beohs, good night cheohs."
We listen to Jeremy till I fall asleep,
after my day of too many notebooks and bus rides
and drizzling raindrops
and too many keys to unlock too many doors
and too many hydrogen atoms
and carbon atoms, which can form 4 covalent bonds
and those change the atom size,
and too much worrying
about mothers and babies and misery and hope.

The last I heard of the story, the turtles had two babies
and all the turtles climbed up
on the backs of the four Billy Goats Gruff
and went back across the bridge and ate waffles.

Jolly comes in and wakes me up,
they're home,
but I don't think I can move,
I stumble to the phone and call my mom and explain
and I spend the rest of the night sleeping with Jilly

till she pulls my nose to tell me,
"It's moehning time, LaVaughn,
get up."

About the kindergarten conference:
"They give a test,
Jeremy did so good on it
they're moving him to a different kidneygarden,
to simulate him.
He has to take his crayons & everything
to a different room.
He'll have to learn a different teacher.
Is that fair, LaVaughn? Well, is it?
See, here's the card they give me."

Sure enough, Jeremy is getting moved to
Advanced Kindergarten
for "greater stimulation and enrichment."

I help the kids get dressed for school,
and I ask Jeremy how he feels about it,
about getting to go in another kindergarten room.
He is all dressed,
putting his story books in a pile
on the floor beside his bed.

"They gots a guinea pig and gerbils
and my friend is there.
They get to do bigger numbers.
Can I still go back and see my real teacher?"

So it's settled.
Jeremy is getting advanced.
Too many thoughts are whirling in my brain,
I kiss the kids goodbye
and we all go to school, including Ricky
who goes to Firefighter Training,
partly paid for by Ricky,
partly by a club of strangers
who worry about the city.

## 50.

The many questions
all gather together into a mass:
How did Jeremy get his hungry brain?
Why do Jolly and Dr. Moore move their arms
just exactly alike?
And why was there something from the very beginning
about Dr. Moore's smile? As if—
as if it is a smile that can suspend itself.
I could never say that about Jeremy's smile
or Jilly's. Their smiles burst out.
Dr. Moore's smile is more—
well, it's bright like glass.

Oh, I should be ashamed. She has put a computer
into my very own life.
She wrote the recommendation letter overnight
for me to get into college
where I have always wanted to go.
I should be ashamed.
There's nothing wrong with her smile.

## 51.

On the other hand:
When she found a kink in the schedule
the next Tuesday afternoon
and we had to go to a different lecture hall,
her face soured,
some kind of current pushing up from inside.

Then she put on that friendly smile again,
but it took some time,
more than a second. More than three seconds.
Anybody could see it.

## 52.

Residential,
ward of the state,
the mother Jolly invented
with the pink everything and the bedroom ruffles,
the adoption picnics, the Box Kids:
These are fragments, shards, pieces.
We're waiting for the bus,
taking Jilly home from Head Start,
with Jeremy jumping small jumps
to keep from being bored,
Jilly standing on my right shoe, swinging from my arm
and singing "Thwee little kittens
they lost theoh mittens. . . ."
I ask Jolly, I can't stop myself,
I whisper over the kids' heads,
almost in Jolly's face:
"Where did you come from, Jolly?"

And I wish I had not done it
the instant the word "from" was out of my mouth
I knew it was too cruel a thing to do.
Jolly shrinks into herself,

trying not to be here,
and as I'm reaching out with my arm
to try to erase my question,
I never before imagined such a soft scream,
I don't think the kids even heard it,
Jolly answers me,
just a small, whispery murmur of a scream,
her neck veins pulsing to show me my mistake:
"I don't KNOW!"

And then she bends over double,
and I wish I could trade her places
so she won't have to be her unknown self
just for this minute
and Jeremy gets his face down under hers,
nosing her up again,
announcing, "I did 47!"
Nothing moves,
everybody stands still.
Jeremy has done 47 small jumps without stopping
and he is telling his mother about them,
panting and happy.

Will this be the thing we'll all remember,
years from now,
when cold days come again?

Or will we remember all this awful weight
of Jolly and her not knowing?
The bus comes, we get on,
I am wishing I could unsay what I said.
We get seated, the bus starts to take us home.

Jeremy and Jilly begin singing:
 *"Ferra zhaka*
 *Ferra shaka*
 *Dormay voo*
 *Dormay voo*
 *Sunny lemon teenas*
 *Sunny lemon teenas*
 *Din din don*
 *Din din don."*

They pull imaginary ropes, ring imaginary bells,
"Din din don, din din don,"
waking up the same sleepyhead
children have been singing to for centuries.

## 53.

These little singing ones don't know it's mystifying,
the topic of who they are.
Their mother had no mother,
she doesn't know her own life story,
but she makes sure they know they have a mother
every day and every night.

And I can't stop, *can't stop* wondering:
Why do Dr. Moore and Jolly move their arms,
slam their books down with a whoosh,
and smile that breakable smile
exactly alike?

Dr. Moore's baby died.
Or not? All my information comes
from the bathroom, I don't know the true facts.
She helps other people's daughters
in memory of her own dead baby.
Or not?
It makes my heart race.

Jolly is 20 years old this year.
I try to picture Dr. Moore 20 years ago.
I think she would have been a medical student
the same age as those I see riding the bus with me
who sometimes go to sleep, their heads lolling
from so many hours of work,
always in their coats or scrubs and name badges,
studying how to heal and cure.

Every time I look at Jolly
I see more small things. The way her mouth gets
when she laughs.
How her feet go up steps, even how she coughs.
Every time I look at Dr. Moore I see such details,
little flares of light come up in my mind
making my eyes dart.

The day Dr. Moore found she had brought
the wrong notebook,
slammed it down on the lectern,
and gave us the enzyme lecture from her memory:
It was the way the notebook hit the wood,
the way Dr. Moore seemed for a tiny instant
to blame the notebook for being the wrong one.
What if I can get Jolly her mother back?
Get Dr. Moore's baby back?

What if?
How would this thing happen?

By testing.
Their DNA.
I probably have Jolly's DNA all over me.
I lend her a sweater here, share a sandwich
or a drinking cup there,
but getting Dr. Moore's DNA?
Impossible. I could never ask her, not in a million years.

How to do this thing in secret?
It is not illegal
but it is dishonest. What kind of girl am I?
Whom to tell? Just to let it out,
this bursting thing that keeps me awake,
pulls my thoughts away in school.
Who would listen?
Myrtle? Annie? Jody? My mom?
Every one of them would have an opinion
to stop me in my tracks.

I wake up in the night,
the streetlight has not been shot out for 3 months,
it shines on my painted weeping willow,
the branches and nest of baby birds

and I have to admit to myself:
There is not a soul I can tell.
I am on my own.
It is so lonely in here, being me and wondering.

I can't go back to sleep
so I go to my laptop and visit DNA again,
the ladder, the chromosomes coiled and uncoiled,
the double helix that Rosalind Franklin photographed
with its skeleton of sugar and phosphate molecules.
The rungs of the ladder are the bases, hydrogen-bonded:
A for adenine,
T for thymine,
G for guanine,
C for cytosine.
C and T are smaller, single-ringed pyrimidines,
always teamed with the larger, double-ringed purines,
G and A.
Our genome, 23 pairs of chromosomes.
The difference a single nucleotide can make.

No two human beings are alike,
just as no two zebras have the same stripes
but the mitochondrial DNA (mtDNA) makes sure
a mother and her offspring have cellular similarities.

Imagine such a detailed wonder of a thing existing
inside human cells.
Three billion chemical base pairs.
Imagine discovering it. Imagine.
Jolly. Dr. Moore. LaVaughn and her questions.


When the alarm buzzes in the morning
a word comes with it:
PATRICK.
Patrick and his lab card.
I could sneak DNA samples from Dr. Moore
and from Jolly.
Couldn't I? Could I?
It's been months since Patrick and I talked on the bus,
standing in the aisle,
backpacks bumping into each other.
That time in the Art Museum doesn't count,
he didn't even see me.
And dreams don't count.
He keeps coming back in them,
always looking in some other direction,
I wake up and shake those dreams away.
Just the side of his face stays vaguely around
coming in when I least expect it.

Patrick.

How could I say the words to him?

*Will you help me extract DNA from stolen samples*
*and do the PCR, help me identify the genetic markers*
*so I can find out if my friend*
*came from where I think she came from?*

It's dishonest

and Patrick would not do something dishonest.

Or would he?

If he knew how important it is?

# 54.

I called his number four times and hung up
before I had enough nerve to face his voice:
So many past reasons for him not to listen to me.

The boy I wouldn't go to a dance with.
The boy I laughed at
because he couldn't spell "Valentine"
when he gave me one.
The boy I disdained, that's what he said.
His smart brain,
the flowers he named in Latin and gave me
on my birthday,
his considering eyes.
His special Academy.
I know too much about Patrick
not to be nervous with him now.

And what I'm going to ask him:
to run the samples without permission
from either Jolly or Dr. Moore.
But how could I not want to give Jolly back her mother,
if she is her mother?

How could I not want to give Dr. Moore back
her daughter,
if she is her daughter?

In the world they are strangers,
but would their cells recognize each other?

A man answers in question marks:
"Huh? Patrick? Yeah, I guess,
I guess I seen him. . . . Maybe yesterday,
you want Patrick?"

Yes, I want Patrick, who finds the note
four days later, dropped on the floor
and a boot mark on it,
but he made sense of "Call Levon."

"Hi, LaVaughn?"
"Hi." My voice quivers.

"Uh, well, uh, how are you?" I start.
The worst beginning.
"Reasonable, I guess."
His brain thinks in such fast speeds
and yet his words are always slow.

"Uh, I want to know if you—
well, I have reasons, I think,
I think—I mean I'm not sure but I think—"

"LaVaughn, take a deep breath," says Patrick.
I stop breathing entirely.
I take a deep breath.
"I wonder if you'll help me do a DNA test. . . .
Uh—extract the DNA.
Load the samples. Do the PCR.
Find the genetic markers. Do the DNA typing. Uh . . ."
Of course the deep breath worked.
I didn't need Patrick to tell me that
although he seems to know more than I do
about everything,
even about breathing.
He is such a special case of smartness
and for a moment I almost drop the whole thing.

Then I start:
"It's because I think two people might be related,
but they don't even know each other,
and I don't want them to know—
I mean, if you think somebody
could be related to somebody,
well, I mean if they move their hands the same way,

they have eyes that could be related,
just a hunch—a good hunch—
but if it doesn't turn out . . .
I mean I don't want to tell them my hunch
I don't want to get them . . ."

I have now told him everything I can.

"You don't want to break their hearts."
I remember like a flash photo
Patrick telling me way back in the biology lab
that the nuns safety-pinned his mittens to his jacket
so he would stay warm in winter.

"That's what I mean," I say.

"Well, it's not against the law," he says.
"But it's not ethical, either."

I knew that already.

"But, listen, Patrick,
what if it turns out they are—
what if it turns out—
And they would never find out

if we don't, I mean if—
So, Patrick, will you help?
Will you help me?"

Patrick says,
"Well, I don't know. . . .
We'd have to go to the U.,
use their genetic analyzer,
they do those analyses all the time,
I've worked on dozens of them with my professor—
but not like this. . . ."

In this silence Patrick calibrates with his big mind,
in this silence I hope with my small one.
I can feel my own pulse, impatient, ready to leap.

"You have the samples?" he says.
No, and the thought of getting Dr. Moore's DNA
in my hands
runs fear through my body head to toe.
"I'll get them," I say.

I hear him start to say something,
then a silence,
like a shadow,

his brain is whirling, I can feel it while I wait.

"I'll get the samples. I'll call you."

"Okay, LaVaughn." Almost as if it is not a yes or no at all.

And we left it there.

I will disrupt, invade,

I will trespass,

I will find out.

Deoxyribonucleic acid.

I did not even ask him How's school at the Academy.

## 55.


Dr. Moore's DNA fills my mind.
Despite this floating double helix
I also have school,
and I go with Annie to her exercise class,
I stretch and bend with her and her growing belly,
we get our neurotransmitters going
and she is almost a good sport about it.
By now she knows:
When you feel panic or despair coming,
you need to flex and twist and reach and bounce,
and her favorite jump rope is in her backpack,
even though the pregnancy teachers say to give it a rest.

And I help Jolly when she calls
and says Jeremy needs new crayons for kindergarten
or Jilly keeps forgetting to bring her mittens home,
and I have laundry up at the Children's Hospital
and my mom makes me eat healthy foods
every night of the week.

Still, morning and evening,
I think about deoxyribonucleic acid.

There is the dishonest LaVaughn in me.
I have always known she was there,
but she usually stays down inside,
maybe waiting her turn?
Waiting to come up and behave like herself?
I don't want to get to know this LaVaughn that well,
I just want to use her for now.
It's not for a bad purpose. Is it?

Don't think about it, LaVaughn.
Just do it.
At Jolly's house I go through her very own private
personal hairbrush
and find four hairs with follicle cells:
Using tweezers, I put them in a plastic bag
and they go into my backpack.

Dr. Moore is in class early on Tuesday,
the subject is careers in medical technology
including public health in faraway places in the world.
I fill 6 notebook pages with facts and question marks
by the time break comes.

I ask her a question,
just something to get a conversation started.
"Dr. Moore, if you're trained in infectious diseases

you could go to far places and work in public health,
where there's malaria?"

"Well, of course you could," she smiles.
"Oh, and three other girls have related questions—
Tell you what, LaVaughn:
Can you stay after class and we'll have tea again?
We'll go down together,
the south end, as before,
we'll chat about this."

After break I'm almost too shaky to take coherent notes,
my mind keeps wandering,
but, as Dr. Moore has told us,
"Focusing our minds is the best favor
we can do for ourselves.
When we can fend off the distractions,
we are beginning to make progress."
The clock on the wall stays on the same minute forever,
and then I look up and it has lurched ahead.
My mind is hopping,
deoxyribonucleic acid rowdy in my brain,
but I keep my body still, in camouflage.

All I need is a cell of her DNA.
One cell.

Down in the cafeteria,
the south end,
my mind is straining with strategy,
how to get her paper tea cup,
watching it on a counter, on a tray, on a table,
in her left hand, in her right hand, at her mouth.
Her cells on the rim of the cup.

We sit at a table, six of us,
Dr. Moore tells us
that physicians and researchers walk past our class
every afternoon
on their way to and from labs,
most of them in long coats
and we should just stop one of them,
ask what kind of work they do, ask them to explain.
"Everyone here knows the WIMS girls,
they'll be friendly. Ask them," she says,
twinkling with helpfulness,
running her hand through her hair.
"You might get invited to one of the labs,
to watch. Remember: We cannot be passive learners
because there is no such thing."

"Who wants refills?" I hear my voice surging,

suddenly too greedy to help everyone.
Three cups come toward me,
and Dr. Moore's is one of them.
I memorize hers on my cafeteria tray.
They tell me the flavors they want,
I walk to the counter, my hands the only steady thing,
the rest of me trembling with fear and guilt.
I pronounce the words for getting tea refills,
and:

I blink, I stare, I bend down close:
In Dr. Moore's cup lies a hair. Two hairs.
They can't be my hairs. They are Dr. Moore's hairs.
Complete with follicle cells, one of the hairs,
both hairs! I can see them clearly.
My entire body jumps internally
but the naked eye could not see this jump.

The man at the counter gives me
a little plastic bag when I ask,
I tuck Dr. Moore's cup inside it,
keeping my fingers away from the rim,
placing the bag with her DNA in it carefully
in my backpack.
I buy Dr. Moore a fresh cup of the kind of tea she likes.

And after I take the tea refills to the table
the words of the conversation float around,
circling me but not landing.
I sit pretending attention,
and in less than five minutes I say I have to go.
I feel as if everyone at the table
everyone in the cafeteria
can see through my backpack
to the plastic bag and the used paper cafeteria cup
containing the most mysterious hair follicle cells
of my life.

It is next to the other plastic bag with Jolly's hairs inside,
riding on my back.
These DNA molecules can't care about pleasure or pain.
And yet. They are a menace like a lit match
in a child's hands.
I walk along like just anybody,
putting one foot in front of the other
away from the hospital into the evening.

## 56.

Of course I can't sleep.
From the streetlight way below,
I can see the tree I painted on my wall and ceiling
with its nest of little birds,
their open mouths
waiting.
In a snip of thought I know what's wrong:
I never painted them a mother.
She has flown away to get them food
but has not returned yet.
She is just on her way
but they have no way of knowing that,
their little neurons are just
doing what they're supposed to do,
their little syrinxes just have their little vibrations going
and they're calling out their hunger into the sky.

I slide out of bed, I get my paint set out of the closet,
and I get a glass of water by just running a slight trickle
so my mom won't wake up
and I turn on the study lamp

and aim it straight up to where those little baby birds
have been waiting for three long years
while I was too ignorant to let their mother come home.
I climb up on my desk, paints in my hand,
the gift from my great-aunts when I was still a child.
I wet the old paints with water,
I paint the mother bird
in the bare sky,
a little distance away from the tree.
She is not any species of bird,
nor are they. These are birds a child would draw.
She is grayish blackish whitish brownish bluish,
she has feet, tailfeathers, eyes, a beak full of worms,
and outspread wings with a white stripe
making her way home as fast as she can
to feed those babies
who can't wait another minute—

She's coming in for a landing,
I get her feet ready to grip the edge of the nest,
I get her bird brain ready to count the babies
making sure they are all still there,
I get her beak ready to drop that food
right into those yammering little throats
and not a drip of paint is drizzling anywhere.

There, babies,
your momma came back,
now just taste those yummy yummy worms—

I watch her flying toward them,
I climb down off my desk, I view her from the doorway,
from the foot of my bed,
I walk around softly,
I notice a blob of gray paint
on the shoulder of my nightshirt
and I nudge it with my thumb, making it worse.

I turn off the study lamp, I get back in bed.
I give my retinas a few moments to get used to the dark
(because the rhodopsin, a protein in the membrane
of the photoreceptor cells,
gets its shape changed by isomerization of retinal
and sends an impulse along an optical nerve to my brain,
and this doesn't happen instantly in humans)
and then I watch that mother bird flying, flying
on wings supported by hollow bones,
aiming for home.

## 57.

It is a Friday. Gray, icy cold,
with soft snowflakes swaying gently down
landing on my gloves.
The kind of snow my mom says my dad used to call
"flakin' real slow." I do not even remember him saying it.
She says these floating flakes always make her
miss him extra.

My backpack is the most important thing in my life today.
As if it is bigger than the city, the world.

I go to the Children's Hospital at 5:00 a.m. to fold laundry
because I will be somewhere else
during my regular folding time after school.
I am on my way to my first class
2 hours and 48 minutes later,
by now the wind has come up,
blowing garbage against the sides of the bus,
and I appear to be a harmless girl.
After school I go to meet Patrick at his Academy,
to go to the U. together.

I listen to myself saying "go to the U."
like an everyday trip.

Underneath the bags in my backpack
I have bananas
to eat when the nervousness hits.
Even just walking from the bus stop to his school
my heart rate begins to go up.
And not just because
it's close to 8.5° Celsius outside.
Well, it takes 1.8 Fahrenheit degrees
to make one Celsius degree,
and all that Summer Science
has made me think in Celsius most of the time.

Patrick's Academy is an old building
that got saved from being destroyed for a parking lot.
Big old trees are on both sides of its brick walkway
and the doors are antique.
Patrick meets me at the north entrance,
as he said he would.
I am on time and so is he, in his blazer and necktie.

Does he keep getting taller
or have I not been paying attention?

When he says Hi it is as if he is asking me something
but I don't know what
and I don't let it distract me.
I think I notice the side of his face is kind of swollen.
Or maybe not. I haven't seen him in months,
my memory has probably gone slack.

"We'll ride the shuttle to the U.," he says,
and even the bus stop at his Academy looks pampered:
It has a roof for shelter from the weather,
and a covered shelf of books and magazines,
one about stars, one about Russian buildings,
one about forests.
A sign says, "Take one, leave one,"
a lending library at their very own bus stop.

One girl on the bus
is going to a dance class, one has a box full of rocks,
a boy has a conference with a professor
about the history of salt.

"You're the one in the picture," says the girl with the rocks.
"Patrick, you hid her till now?"
I could ask, "Where? What picture? Of me?"

That is all too complicated,
with such cargo in my backpack
and those bags in my mind
and I see his face really is swollen.
The left side.

I look out the window instead,
pretend I don't have this loaded backpack,
pretend it is next year,
me in a different sweater, new boots,
a mature college student sitting in this bus seat,
going places
with thick books in my pack,
and understanding what's in their pages.
This is the very same City University
I saw from the bus window with Jody
when we went to the Museum
and Patrick didn't look at me.
High above the street is the sign:
LET KNOWLEDGE SERVE THE CITY.
Its brass letters shine out through the gray, snowy rain.
College students are throwing snowballs,
building snow statues
in big groups, small groups, alone,

laughing, shouting, hats falling off,
and two girls sit together on a bench in the snow, crying.

The bus lets us off in the midst of the crowd,
we walk along in their bootprints,
nobody looks at me, nobody tells me I don't belong.
We get to one of the science buildings, take an elevator,
a sky bridge, and about eight turns
and in front of a solid metal door that says
"Molecular Biology Lab C"
Patrick takes out a card,
puts it in a small slot, a small green light flashes,
and he turns the knob.

"You really do have a key. You said you had a card.
It's a key—
Patrick, you've got a real key. . . ."

"It's just to this lab.
It's not a big—"
But the door opens, the sanitized lab smell comes at us,
and he says, "Well, yes, it is a big deal. It is.
I'm a lab assistant here."
We are almost laughing together
as we used to, way back at school

when Patrick had only a ragged sweatshirt
and we studied for quizzes neck and neck.
But I can't relax enough for a genuine actual laugh.
We are in a molecular biology lab at the U.
where he is a real lab assistant
and the door closes behind us.

# 58.

Through a door I see the genetic analyzer
in its clean, isolated room,
a machine that would make Gregor Mendel's heart jounce.
I have read about this invention
and I recognize it 30 feet away,
a throne of smartness that looks like a refrigerator.
(Sometimes couldn't you just jump up and down
to celebrate electricity? I could.)

This machine automates DNA sequencing.
Even one room away from it
I get weak knees, wavy brain.
Can Jolly get a mother out of this machine?
This is not a crazy question.

We take off our coats,
Patrick turns on the ultra-violet light
in one of the fume hoods
to sanitize everything inside it.
In this rich lab are thermocyclers,
microcentrifuges in four sizes, three different hoods,
inverse and dissecting microscopes, two autoclaves,

two incubators, refrigerators, freezers,
two liquid nitrogen holding tanks,
equipment my school could only imagine.
And chemicals. Shelves and shelves of them.

I set my pack on a lab stool,
I pull out the two little bags, lay them on the counter,
try to pretend these hair shafts look innocent.

Patrick holds the bags up to the light,
separately and together,
and says in his slow way,
"You had permission to take these?"
I say no.
He tilts his head to one side.
His face actually is swollen. There's a scab.
"LaVaughn, you really can't do that."

I can't figure out a way to be ashamed
and I tell him so. "Patrick, I have to know.
They have to know. If they're related."
He continues looking at me, his opinion in his eyes.

"Or not," I say.

He folds his arms, leans both elbows on the lab counter,

looks at the plastic bags,
looks at me,
puts his forehead down on the counter
as if he's going to pray or sleep.

"Patrick, if you knew—" I say to his back,
"Just— If you knew—
the possibility . . ."

He doesn't move,
he says into the lab counter,
"Do you think I go through a day in my life
without wondering about possibility?
LaVaughn." The words are slow, as always.

Even bent over,
eyes closed, his swollen face on the counter,
his betterness comes across the space between us
as simply as Jilly walking into a room.
Patrick is always nicer than I am; smarter, of course,
has had a harder life,
he stands up straight again.
"Well, LaVaughn," he shakes his head,
"I don't know."
In the plastic bags

Jolly's and Dr. Moore's cells lie waiting.

"You took somebody's coffee cup.
This is— LaVaughn, you really can't do this."

"I've done it, Patrick," I say, my voice as quiet as his.
"Patrick, you said. You said."

He looks at my hands.
"Well— Well, it was an impulse.
I hadn't thought through it.
LaVaughn, you phone me out of the blue sky,
you ask me to do something for you,
we worked together for a whole year in school,
and Summer Science—"
I watch his mouth being right about me being wrong.
His eyes don't flinch,
he keeps going.
"Then poof. Nothing.
One day on a bus, a minute, two minutes,
then you're gone again.
Then you're not.
You caught me off-guard, LaVaughn,
I thought you'd forgotten my name."

I change the weight of my body to my other foot.
He does the same thing,
we stand still, arguing with our cheek muscles.
"It isn't right, LaVaughn."

The Guidance Man is in my ears so loudly
I can't stop him:

> **. . . you know the difference between right and wrong,
> and you act in accordance with your conscience,
> using that insight.**

I take a banana out of my backpack,
it's not as discolored as it might be,
I open it and take a bite,
I need the potassium in my bumbling stomach,
then I hold it out to Patrick,
he takes a chunk and puts it in his mouth.
I speak up over the voice of the Guidance Man:
"This is something bigger, Patrick.
I can't tell you who—"

"I don't want you to—"

"But I think it *is* right."
In the silence I see Jolly
walking away from the adoption picnic

with $15 to get her through her life.

"It's real important to you, isn't it?" he says.
"Real important," I answer, not letting my voice burst,
not letting my eyes go wild
holding people's lives in my mind
and almost not breathing.

He goes to a shelf of books,
pulls out an instruction manual,
looks at the date, says it's from last year, puts it back,
pulls out another one, checks the index,
lays it on the counter.

He opens a cabinet door, gets us each a lab coat,
goes to drawers, pulls out a box of sterile PCR tubes,
microcentrifuge tubes, a 96-well plate,
micropipettes, a box of pipette tips,
puts out a box of sterile gloves.
He puts all these in the hood.
We are in our lab coats, we are gloved.
Everything we do inside the hood
will look bluish.
Back in Summer Science
the teachers made sure we respected the hood
and some students even saluted it when they walked past.

Patrick looks around the lab, studies the hood
where we'll work. "Any contamination
and the work is lost." I know this already,
but hearing him say it hints
he will probably help me till we're done.

He puts forceps and scalpels in a countertop sterilizer.
He opens the instruction manual, checks two places in it,
puts it back on the counter,
then discards the gloves he's wearing and takes a new pair.

He picks up the bag with Dr. Moore's tea cup
and its prize lucky hairs with follicle cells attached.
"We're gonna use an alkaline solution, clean these up
for better amplification," he says in his slow way.
I label the sample tubes,
Dr. Moore is sample A and Jolly is sample B,
and Patrick and I are shoulder to shoulder,
our gloved hands in the hood.

He reaches into the bag with forceps, lifts out one hair,
cuts off the follicle cells with the scalpel,
cuts the hair into fragments one centimeter long
and divides them between two microcentrifuge tubes,
smaller than the end of my smallest finger.
I copy him exactly with Jolly's hair follicle cells,

dividing between two tubes
so we'll have duplicates just in case.

We add to each tube a drop of sterile buffer
and we puree the hair shafts
with a tissue homogenizer
so the genomic DNA can be released.
Patrick's hands are calm,
mine are not.

We follow the instruction manual word by word:
Patrick reads each step to me
and then I read it back to him.
Ethanol, proteinase k, lysis buffer, sterile water
in exact proportions
in tubes that hold 1.5 milliliters,
teensy and unforgettable in our hands.

Now we are ready to lyse. Lysis means breaking apart;
chemical buffers break apart the fatty cell membranes
to let DNA out. We pipette the buffers into the tubes,
Patrick's hand guides the micropipette as easily as a pencil,
my hand keeps wanting to shake,
I brace my elbow on the counter.
Each measurement is in microliters,
and we vortex the tubes in the microcentrifuge

after each addition. Whirling these lives,
as if we had the right to.

All hair fragments are submerged in proteinase k;
we hold the tubes, we flick them with our fingers
to help the mix,
and the only words we say
are "vortex" and "here" and "OK" and "yes."
We put the solutions on a rocking platform at 55° Celsius,
and Patrick sets it for two hours.

## 59.

We take off the gloves,
we sit down, I swing my legs,
looking like just somebody sitting in a lab,
a warm place on a winter day.
I want to ask him about his swollen face,
but first things first:
"Patrick, do you know where you came from?"
When I asked Jolly
I jumbled her so badly
she shrank down with the impact.

He looks straight at me. "No."
He simply says no.
Pushy LaVaughn goes on: "What if—
what if you had the chance, what if you could get,
get a tea cup or . . . You've got this whole lab—
just on a hunch, or—
What if you could find out?"

He picks up a micropipette, looks at it in his hand,
puts it back down on the counter,
looks at me, looks down at his hands,

looks up at me again.

"All I know is she didn't want me bad enough to keep me.
She must of wanted me to go away.
That's enough to know."
Sitting there with his lumpy face,
his mouth does not bend,
he must have learned as a small child
not to let this make him cry.
How did he learn that?

I say, "But maybe she had to. Maybe she wanted you
and just couldn't—"

"I don't want to see her face, LaVaughn.
I don't want to know
who did such a thing.
She could of found a way
if she wanted to."
He looks off, away, at a row of cabinets,
at the top of the thermocycler,
at my boots.

I imagine someone seventeen years ago,
her baby in her hands,
giving him into other pairs of hands,
rows of hands,

passing the baby along
and along and along
and he is here on a lab stool
within arm's length of a thermocycler,
a full-grown boy with brain enough for three people,
a slow talker, a fast thinker,
a boy doing a favor for me
even though he thinks it's wrong.

"It would just make a mess.
People getting mad,
making up excuses—
I don't want to know."

Does Jolly want to know?

"It's the nuns I'm glad about," he says.
"They still remember my birthday."
I smile about the nice nuns I never met.
He continues remembering them:
"They let me watch a lot of nature on TV.
I saw animals that never knew they even had a mother.
Things that fly in the air,
things that swim at the bottom of the sea.
They go along, they live their lives."

"You're not a lower life-form, Patrick."

He seems not to hear me say this.
"And nobody else called me by my name,
only the nuns."

"What did other people call you?"

"Oh, in one foster home I was Spud.
In a different one I was Little Guy.
Where I live now they call me Chucker.
It's never because the name fits,
it's always just the first thing somebody thinks of."

I wonder how he wakes up every morning
and goes through a day.
"Want me to show you around?" he asks.
"Sure," I say,
and we slide off our stools
and go to one of the microscopes,
he lifts off the cover and puts up a slide of a cell,
blue and green and purple like an exotic flower.
"Hey, that's mitosis!" I say, startled.
"Yeah, metaphase," he says next to my forehead.
This must be an extra extra-fancy microscope
and Patrick gets to do this stuff whenever he wants to.

But I know who my mother is and she cooks me supper
and I sit down and eat it out of habit.

He's getting another slide out
and I have the nerve to ask,
"Patrick, what's the swelling on your face about?
That lump. Right there," I point to his left jaw.

"It's nothing," he says.
"You should see a doctor," I say.
"It's nothing," he says.
"I don't believe that," I say.
"I got in a fight." Not mumbled, but in an undervoice.
"Really?"
"I said I got in a fight. Of course really."
"What about?" I ask. I did not think Patrick
would be a fighter.

His eyes change just slightly,
he gets a measuring look in them.
"I hit the guy that lost your phone message."
"You hit somebody just because he's a jerk?"
I can't help asking.

"Not just because." He fits the syllables together
piece by piece.

"Now we've got kitchen duty for three weeks.
Together. They say it's to see if we think
we're too big to learn social responsibility."

He holds a slide between two fingers,
lifting it toward the lens so I can look at it.
Patrick with his extreme brain
lives in lost and found places
and he is sent to the kitchen
to learn social responsibility.
There is nothing secret about this
and yet it feels as if I've just received something.

I don't know what it is.

He puts the slides back in their case
and moves toward our tubes of DNA.

He got that big lump because of me.
Because Jolly needs a mother.
Because LaVaughn needs Patrick.
I have never known a boy who would hit somebody
about me.

"So I am a lower life-form," he says.

"No, you're not," I say. "No, you're not."
I said it twice because I didn't know what else to say.

He checks the hair follicle cells in their tubes and says,
"You want to see more of the building?"
I say yes. I have to keep busy with something,
anything to distract me from those tubes.

We put our lab coats and gloves
in contamination bins,
Patrick locks our backpacks in a cabinet,
and we leave.

"That's Insect Biology," he points through an open door
and we go in, two girls tell us
they're studying lady beetle migration.
The whole place would be Jeremy's idea of a good time,
insects in tanks everywhere.
Going down the hall we see the botany section,
an entire lab devoted to fungus,
on a different floor
we pass four labs of cancer cell research,
and we get to the end of the building
where we go out on a balcony
looking down on the snowy campus,

skinny tree branches dropping snow globs,
people tramping to and fro.

This is the U.
This is where you detach yourself
from your childhood ignorance
and your new knowledge crowds in
and grows you up.

If I could go to school here.
If I could.
I even whisper it
but I don't think Patrick hears me.

## 60.

Back in the overprivileged lab—
in fresh lab coats and gloves—
we are ready to collect DNA.

We add ethanol,
we vortex again in smaller tubes,
we pipette the mixture into minicolumns
inside collection tubes,
so little they look like toys.
Again, I watch Patrick's hands,
how he centers things
so no ethanol strays outside the minicolumn.
We centrifuge these tubes for 60 seconds,
we throw away the collection tubes,
we get new ones,
we add a different buffer, we centrifuge again,
we repeat the process.
Each time we discard the collection tubes
we're throwing away proteins, cellular debris,
fragments of two lifesize people
like letters we've decided not to mail.

We put the minicolumn in a new microcentrifuge tube
and pipette a different buffer
directly onto the membrane inside.
Incubate for 60 seconds, centrifuge for 60 seconds,
add buffer and do it again.
This last part is elution,
where larger molecules flow fast off a surface
and smaller molecules take a longer time.
Elution isolates the DNA from everything else,
and we do it three times,
each time in a clean collection tube.
In this extreme filtering
we turn our backs on everything that is not useful to us,
sneaking up on the evidence like bloodhounds.

# 61.

"We're gonna quantify the DNA," says Patrick.
This quantifying is new to me.
He pipettes some of sample A
into the small black cuvette,
which looks like a miniature skyscraper
but fits between his two fingers,
and puts it in the spectrophotometer
(I memorize the name),
he presses the dilution factor signal,
and the numbers come up quickly.

"Ha! Sample A, great," he says. Sample B goes in
and I stand on tiptoe for good luck.
"Sample B, great too," he says,
and now some of me relaxes
for the first time since the nervy beginning.
If we hadn't got enough DNA from either sample
I would have had to start over from the start.
Would I have done that? The cafeteria, the tea cup?
Would I?

I stand back in wonder:
The hairs of two people happening to be in the world,
the pouring and pipetting, the lysing and measuring,
the lighting up of numbers on small screens.

And that is that. DNA ready to match.

## 62.

Next is the polymerase chain reaction,
PCR. This is a way to break apart the DNA double helix
that is coiled tightly inside the nucleus of our cells.
Well, except red blood cells don't have any DNA.
All our other cells do.
When I was a young girl
my teacher hollered on my paper
in great big purple pen:

> *RIGHT LAVON! Red blood cells*
> *does not have DNA. How come*
> *nobody ELSE got this question right in*
> *the whole class?*

If you uncoiled a DNA molecule
it would be almost six feet long.
Our cells are always making copies of themselves,
and here's how: The DNA double helix
is like a ladder with rungs.
Just picture a rope ladder,
coiled up.
It keeps replicating itself as long as we live:

The sides of the ladder unzip
and separate into two strands.
The ladder rungs match up
with their right partners and make new daughter strands,
and then they are a new double helix,
but each one is half parent and half child.
Now name the rungs their right name: nucleotides.
There are only four kinds,
adenine, cytosine, guanine and thymine.

The nucleotides can match up
with only one kind of partner:
A's and T's pair up, C's and G's pair up,
according to the recipe that lives in the memory of cells,
and each couple is called a base pair. That's one rung.
We've all got 3 billion base pairs.

PCR in a lab imitates this copying
by temperature cycling.
We heat the DNA to 95° Celsius
to break the hydrogen bonds
(it's called denaturing),
and the rungs unzip to form half ladders,
we spike the mix with primer
for the enzymes to stick to,
then we cool it to 55° (it's called annealing),

and add enzymes from bacteria that live in hot springs,
and we add nucleotides,
then we heat it again
and the enzymes can read
the A's and T's, C's and G's
and we add matching nucleotides
and a new copy of DNA gets made
and that's the extension.
Denaturing, annealing, extension.
An everyday rule of molecular biology.

It goes on every moment in every life-form,
it sounds so simple,
and yet millions of years of life on earth went by
before Kary Mullis figured it out in 1983
and ten years later
the Nobel Prize in Chemistry came to him.

We will end up with genomic DNA
from these essential pinhead-size polymers,
these blobs of keratin, these long chains of amino acids
that we got from human hair.
If:
If we have enough uncontaminated DNA,
if we get the right combination of chemicals
into the DNA samples,

if the chemicals have been stored at −20° Celsius,
if we do the protocol precisely in every detail.

With the plate in the thermocycler at 94° Celsius
we take off our gloves and we'll wait.

The door opens. In walks a man in a long lab coat,
wearing a badge like Patrick's,
carrying a large cardboard box and whistling.

"Hi, Patrick. Checking your nematodes, are you?" he says,
walking along past us. He puts the box on a lab counter.

"No, not yet, sir," says Patrick.
"This is LaVaughn, we're doing some PCR.
Her school doesn't have the equipment."

The man and I say hello and he is not at all excited
about my excellent handshake.
"Hmm, yes," he says,
looking past Patrick into the hood.
"Cleaned up after yourselves, did you?"
"Of course, sir," says Patrick.
I do not move, I keep my eyes on the genetic analyzer
in case this sir can see by looking at me

that I am doing something so wrong, wrong, wrong
to two people of my life. Even though it is right.

He walks around two counters
to the other side of the room,
pulls out drawers, pushes them back in,
and leaves the lab,
still whistling.

"Want to see my nematodes?" Patrick asks me.
Sure, I say. He shows me his petri dishes
where worms have been feeding on insect larvae.
These nematodes have a very short lifespan,
about three days
and they have about 100 base pairs,
not many at all.
We look at them wriggling
under the dissecting microscope
which I remember how to use
because of Summer Science.
Patrick adds more insect larvae, adjusts the water,
records his data in a notebook
and puts them all away for next time.

We put on clean gloves

and we are standing in front of the genetic analyzer.
I almost bow down to it.
Capillary electrophoresis. It is the most modern thing
I have ever seen.
Patrick says "electrokinetic injection" as easily
as I would say "lunchtime" or "Jeremy's glasses."

Inside this machine is an array of hair-thin capillary tubing
arranged in an arch 50 centimeters long,
and as the DNA molecules—the amplicons—
move through them
a laser detector sees how fast the amplicons are moving.
Amplicons are genetic markers that will show
in an electropherogram on a computer screen,
and Patrick knows how to read them.
I listen to him saying
"deoxyribonucleoside triphosphate" and I laugh.
He goes silent
and I know with a jolt that I've done it again.
I am not the first girl ever to laugh at a really smart person:
Finding something funny about them
makes the rest of us feel not quite so unsmart
for a moment
but doing it shows how unsmart we are.
I watch his eyes going away
and say to myself I knew better

but ignored what I knew.

Without a word, Patrick loads our samples in the wells
along with the control (no DNA in it),
and we'll wait for the electrical current
to pull the DNA through
past the laser detector. It will take nearly 24 hours.

"We'll find out tomorrow," he says.
Under his voice
something is stretched or trampled or tearing
or already torn.

# 63.

We take off the gloves,
I put my coat on
as if I were going on a long trip.
I am standing in a university lab
where my friend and my teacher
are in capillary tubing in a genetic analyzer
without their permission
and inches away from me is a boy
helping me do this
who doesn't know where he came from
and I keep insulting him.

He picks up his pack
and I try to repair a little:
"Patrick, will you show me around your Academy?"
He looks at me,
the measuring look he uses in living his life.
"Maybe tomorrow? Before we come here to the lab . . ."
I'm hoping my voice sounds like that of a nice person.

"You want to see it?" he asks, no tone at all in his voice.

"Yes. I do."

"Okay," he says, no tone.

I brought him stolen hair follicle cells,
he got his face smashed because of me,
people in foster homes don't bother to learn his name,
and I laughed at him.

We are like eggshells, Patrick and I.
We'll begin again the next day.
I take a different bus home.

## 64.

At home are clean towels
fish and sauce for dinner
bad news from out in the world
and my mother
saying her upset opinions about it, doing her job
of bringing me up right.

To avoid the heebiejeebies
about everything
I take a hot bubble bath
and I look where my mom has patched the grout
around the tub
so the insects won't crawl out of the wall
into our own personal water.
I lie back, popping bubbles two by two:
Soap molecules, water molecules, hydrocarbon chains,
decreased surface tension
entertaining me.

After homework I lie in my bed looking up

at the mother bird, always carrying, always bringing.
In the lab those DNA amplicons
are moving through the capillary tubing.
I get the heebiejeebies whether I want to or not.

## 65.

Snow has drifted into humps and mounds,
three inches of pillowy white
and I am up early enough this Saturday morning
to see the city calm, quiet, waiting underneath
before the soot and muddy mush take over.

Jolly's DNA amplicons
and Dr. Moore's. Across the city
in Molecular Biology Lab C at the U.
I camouflage my jitters, something I am getting
so good at.

At Patrick's Academy
a huge metal sculpture sways over the snow
high as the second-floor windows,
and this morning it is roofed in white,
modern art hanging over ancient earth.

Patrick meets me as he said he would
but he gives me only a sideways view
of him and his bruised face,
hardly any conversation

as he shows me the gym
where about twenty people are dancing in leotards,
and huge, high classrooms that smell of old wood,
with creaky floors and windows that rattle in the wind.
These old rooms have brand-new everything:
thick books, modern chairs, computer screens,
big pots of plants,
bright lights, straight shelves,
electronic inventions everywhere.

We look in silence,
this boy of few words and me, standing like a stick,
embarrassed
and wondering why I even suggested coming here.

We walk down a hallway and make three turns,
and by surprise:
"Well, here's my office—" he says.
We have toured through rooms and rooms,
he has barely spoken
and now this: cubicle, desk, computer,
two shelves of books, a cushioned chair,
his name in a frame on the wall,
I gawk.

"We can't use the excuse

that home isn't a good place to study,
so they give everybody an office," he says,
sounding more like his usual self.

On his desk is a note on a torn notebook page:

> *Patrick, You going to ArtGames Sunday?*
> *If yes we want you on our team. Terry & Nicole.*

Another one on pink paper:

> *Patrick—Did you get the laser diode question?*
> *With the controlled constant current*
> *transconductance?*
> *Share your results? —Rosemary M.*

He moves them both a few inches.
"The controlled constant current transconductance
has to be amplified," he says, picking up a pen
and starting to write on the pink page.
I can't help laughing.
Or I tell myself later I couldn't have helped it.

He stops writing, looks at me,
decides something with his eyes,

puts the pen on the desk
and raises his voice just a small amount.
"Listen, LaVaughn. You keep laughing at me, you—"

"But I'm not laughing at—"
"You don't get it about me, LaVaughn,
you don't get it a bit. I'm gonna tell you.
Just listen."

I blink and go alert.
"I told you about the nuns,
how they . . .
Another thing they did:
I stammered real bad, they made me slow down.
Every time I said words
I had to stretch them out in my mind,
like a car slows down,
they played a nature movie in slow motion,
with a heron flying slow over a valley,
I had to say
'her   on   fly   ing   slow   ov   er   the   val   ley,'
they made me say it a hundred times
to make sure I'd get the point.
I was a five-year-old
telling everybody about the heron, how slow it flies.

We had treats and candy at the orphanage on Sunday,
they wouldn't let me have any if I talked too fast."

He kept looking straight at me
till he got to the treats and candy,
then he looked away.
He is right. I did not get it at all.
Every time he opens his mouth
he has to put all that quantity of thinking
slowly through a teensy, narrow funnel.
"I didn't know that," I say,
"I didn't know it, Patrick,"
and I look him straight in the face
while I am trying to push the blame away
and failing.

Nothing moves.
"You never asked."
He picks up the pen again
and answers Rosemary M. on the paper,
bending over in the light, misspelling "amplified"
and pushing the note to the side of his desk.
I never asked. I never asked at all.

## 66.

I devote myself
to thinking of the right thing to say.
Or anything.

And now I see the photo of me on his bulletin board
from back in Summer Science
in the costume of a monk of the 19th century
holding a pea plant in one hand
and a chart of hereditary traits in the other.
I was pretending to be the discoverer Gregor Mendel
instead of the mostly ignorant girl I really was.

And next to the photo
in big red letters on another paper:
HELPING HANDS TO AFRICAN HOSPITALS DEADLINE
with his name and a summer schedule
and a list of hospitals
in places I don't know how to pronounce.
"Patrick, this African Hospitals deadline—
Is that you?"

Telling me his childhood stammer,
holding it out for me to catch that way,
unweights the air in here,
my hands don't feel as wrong.
He says, "Well, yeah, it's six weeks,
the hospitals need everything,
me and some others get to go,
just carrying boxes, probably,
and holding babies,
stacking equipment,
but, you know, at least it's something."
"You're going to Africa?" I repeat myself.

"Yeah. People walk hundreds of kilometers
to see doctors.
At least it's something."
Patrick. To Africa.
To hold babies and stack boxes.

He looks at his watch.
It's time to go to the lab.

As we walk out
he translates Latin words on doorways,
*Alimenti*, the cafeteria,

*puellae* on the girls' bathroom.
It feels different now,
I know why he talks that way,
he knows I know,
I teeter on the edge of apologizing.

But we are on our way
to measure the velocity of those amplicons
and I walk along
just as though they were not roaring in my head.

## 67.

Only two other people are on the bus,
both with ice skates.
They invite Patrick to go to the rink
and he says no, he's going to the lab.
"You're always in that lab," says one of them.
When they get off the bus
Patrick tells me a fact of his life:
"I got ice skates for Christmas, we all got them,
I was real little,
I didn't know what they were.
The Sisters took us ice skating
and by the end of the afternoon
I made it all the way around the rink
without falling down."

I think back on my little ice skating hopes
with Myrtle and Annie,
when we wanted to be skating princesses.
I kind of smile sideways at Patrick,
he was probably very cute

learning to ice skate with the nuns.
But my mind is on nucleotides,
chromosomes, genetic markers
and the bus is getting closer to them every moment.

## 68.

In the lab Patrick sits at the keyboard
beside the genetic analyzer,
he types and clicks, types and clicks,
I pull up a chair, my brain whirls
on this precipice of finding out,
and the DNA sequence appears on the screen.
"See, the nucleotides are in colors," he says,
and the dye pattern is clear:
Cytosine is blue, thymine is red,
guanine is black, adenine is green. Across the screen
they advance
in peaks and valleys,
AAATTGTTATCCCCTCACAATT,
"not too much baseline noise here," says Patrick
and he clicks his tongue and nods his head
at the signal intensity numbers.

He scrolls the screen along, he clicks,
he brings up the genetic markers, he studies,
flexing, nodding his head, shaking his head,
saying "Huh?" and "Oh!" and "Yeah, that's—
No, wait a minute— No, yes— Yes, that's it. HPRTB.

And there's the triplex,
CSF1PO on chromosome 5, TP0X on chromosome 2,
TH01 on chromosome 11."
Over his shoulder I read the configurations:
F13A01, FESFPS, vWA,
D16S539, D7S820, D13S317. HPRTB, F13B, LPL
on their proper chromosomes. And the numbers:
9, 8,  9, 8.
6, 5,  6, 5.
11, 11,  11, 10.
11, 9,  12, 11, they line up in close partners
announcing to all the world
what nobody in the world knows yet.


"It looks like you're right, LaVaughn.
See the combined maternity index,
98.78%."
I stare through these markers
at the mother and daughter behind them,
their eyes watching and waiting,
their bones and muscles and skin and brain.


"LaVaughn. You've gotta breathe out sometime—"
I do it.
"So: You're happy now?
This is what you wanted?"

He turns and looks at my face. Can he see the
leaping thrill
ambivalence
confusion
immobilizing fear?

Dr. Moore and Jolly are mother and daughter.
Somebody did kidnap Jolly.
Or— Or what?
My stomach is rising and falling like a boat.
"Uh, it's suddenly more complicated than—
Oh, I don't know what—"

"But it's what you wanted."
"I know. I just didn't know . . ."

Patrick scrolls back
to the red, blue, green, and black peaks.
And up walks another person behind us
in a long lab coat and friendly face.
"Hi, Patrick. I saw your nemotodes over there," she says.
"I just want to make sure you've set them up in triplicate."

Patrick says yes, he did, and he introduces me
and I shake her hand.
"Fine handshake you've got there,"

she says. She points over Patrick's shoulder to the screen:
"You must've gotten good templates, Patrick.
Look at those clear peaks,
your baseline is good, not much noise begins
till way over here,
and that always happens,
we always lose resolution the farther it goes.
Good job, kids! What project is this?"

I hold my breath.
"Uh, this is LaVaughn's,
they don't have equipment at her school. . . ."

"Glad we can share the wealth, then.
Good day, boys and girls." She turns,
jingles some keys and walks away.
Patrick prints the results, three copies.

Patrick, the child of haphazard chance and risk,
dropped off, picked up, shrugged about,
and me, the meddling, busybody girl
who couldn't let this chance pass her by.
I am very struck dumb.
In my mind is Dr. Moore's complicated smile
beaming from one side of the lecture hall to the other.
Although I have thought so many times

what to do now,
I don't know
what to do now.
Slide the lab report under her door?
Put it in her hand after class?
Imagine her smile
as she would take the paper I put in her hands,
and then what would happen to her face.
I can't imagine.

March Jolly up to Dr. Moore and say:
"Your daughter did not die.
And here she is."

Say to Jolly, "I've found your mother,
and wait till you see her."

Put them together in a room
with these DNA charts and see what happens.

Can I do any of those things?

Was Jolly kidnapped?
Remember what Patrick said: "She didn't want me
bad enough."

Dr. Moore did not want her daughter bad enough?
Her daughter became a ward of the state.
I don't understand any of it.
"Thank you, Patrick. I don't know
what I'm gonna do now.
Not at all."

"Tinkertoys," Patrick says.
"What?"
"They did it with Tinkertoys. Watson & Crick
put together the first double helix model with Tinkertoys
because that's what they had.
Use what you have." He puts his finger on my forehead.
"Use that," he says.
We put on our coats.

In this late afternoon
the snow is melting, settling
and stars are out.
I'm ready to say goodbye and stop all thought,
get on the bus
go home and fall down on my bed.

Patrick stands on the sidewalk, looking up.
"The universe," he says.

"100 billion galaxies—
and every one of them's got a trillion stars.
A trillion.
And you know every time a planet comes close to a star
it causes the star to wobble? That's so logical."
He keeps looking up.
"Hydrogen, helium.
And there might even be amino acids out there."

He can't come close to spelling "spectrophotometric,"
but he can read hundreds of small markings on a cell,
thousands of lights in the night sky.

"Thanks, Patrick," I say,
and I walk toward the bus
with such a dangerous document in my pack.

# 69.

The lab report in my backpack
appears to be 2 dull sheets of paper
with letters and numbers,
it goes everywhere with me
for six days.
I don't see Jolly, I pretend I live in a distant place.

In WIMS I listen to the lectures,
I do the labs.
I could just not do anything at all.
Dr. Moore would go on as before.
Jolly would go on as before.
I could choose that way. I could.

I have never been so ambivalent in my life.

I ask myself walking to and from the bus,
folding laundry at the Children's Hospital,
hurrying from class to class in school,
waiting in the lunch line,
watching Myrtle tuck inside Annie's lunch

a note saying "We beleive in you Annie"
or some other big-hearted thought.

Dr. Moore is explaining to us the cranial nerves,
showing them on the big screen.
In order to watch where she points
I'm using the optic, the oculomotor,
the trochlear, the ophthalmic, and the abducens nerves.
These nerves are how I perceived Jeremy
touching my shoelace the day I met him.
Not yet three, he reached down to my foot
with his little hand.
Other nerves make me remember how it was,
how it felt, how he looked up at me, checking
to see if I was the person attached
to the shoelace he was stroking.

I can't not bring these people together.
I can't not.
The lab report lives in my backpack while I try to think.
I'm walking quickly with Annie to her exercise class
and we see Jolly on the sidewalk,
lugging all the boots and jackets
and large paper art work
from Head Start and kindergarten,
and both kids are pulling on her,

each of them needing something right this instant
and Annie says, "Jolly, how do you do it?
How do you do all that—" She points to the two children.

Jolly is not in a mood to be interviewed.
"*Do* it? I *do* it, that's how.
How do I do it?
You ain't got any brain,
you ask that question." She is chasing
Jilly's hair ribbon that has just blown out of her hand.

Annie's body takes a step backward,
her belly following her legs
as if it doesn't quite know how,
being not like itself anymore.

"I do it. There ain't a how.
I just do it."
She trots away with the children
and now I know where she got her gumption.
This gaping fact strains to get out.

I'm tired from holding in.
I have too many secrets for one seventeen-year-old person
to carry around.

## 70.

But what if Jolly was not kidnapped?
What if Dr. Moore . . .

I would lose the computer.
The computer I have come to love.
Dr. Moore's college recommending letter:
she would take it back.
I would get removed from WIMS,
kicked out with my notebooks full of knowledge,
and I would never get to go anywhere.

I would be done for.
Over.
No college, no good job,
I would spend my years in janitorial,
a mop in my hands.

Or would she be grateful?
Has she always wanted to know about her baby?
Who would not?

*71.*

In the immense night in my bedroom
I think back over my life.
How I happened to happen into the world.
The chances of sperm to egg to human heartbeat.

Car horns honk way down on the street.
Human life: honking, honking
wanting everything to go our way.

I have weighed everything I can think of about it.
My mom has no idea in the morning
when I walk out of the house:
I am risking everything I have counted on
since I first sat on the kitchen stool and asked her
if I could ever go to college.
I was a small child then and knew nothing.

The way I do it is not interesting.
I lie to my nervous system,
pretending the envelope is merely an envelope,
I give Dr. Moore the envelope with the lab report inside it

after class
and I walk away. As I expected,
she smiles her alert smile when I put it in her hand.
My stomach nearly regurgitates.
In with the lab report is my note
that says I know the girl with the related DNA,
she is my friend,
and I will introduce them to each other
if Dr. Moore wants me to.

Everything is wrong with the way I did it.
Think of Dr. Moore in her office
which I have never seen.
Think of her sitting in an important chair,
leaning back, relaxing
to read something from a student she likes.
Think of that.

And I did everything else wrong:
Letting Dr. Moore choose to see Jolly or not.
Not telling Jolly first.
Doing it at all.
Everything is wrong with the way I did it.
It is Tuesday.

## 72.

And to the outside world this is merely Wednesday.
A note hangs with my WIMS lab coat,
I am woozy and off-balance with sleeplessness,
even my ears and toes are tired from worry,
but I am good at covering this up by now.
I am 17 and have experience with concealment.

I take the note to the bathroom
and read it in a stall.
In the bathroom they're saying,
"Dr. Faleen wasn't going to lecture till next week,
how come she's doing it today?"
Rushing water covers the answer.

**LaVaughn, See me in my office after class.**
The note goes in my pocket
and I eat the 8th banana in 24 hours.

Dr. Moore is nowhere to be seen.
I take my seat as if I am someone else,
My notes look like my handwriting

but I almost don't feel my hand
drawing the curves and angles of them.
Dr. Faleen tells us her job is
"to do the baby part of the course.
Here is where we can coo all we want
because we all agree, don't we, babies are adorable?"
Every head nods, the automatic dimmers dim the lights,
and she starts the film,
beginning with egg and sperm. She says,
"The transformation from a pair of microscopic gametes
to a human being who can think
and play chess and basketball
is the most amazing cellular process of all. Agreed?"
We agree.
Behind me someone whispers,
". . . poor Dr. Moore who lost her baby,
that must be why we have Dr. Faleen for this part—
You notice Dr. M. never mentions babies?"
Almost rigid in my chair, I try to keep every muscle still.

Dr. Faleen says, "This is mostly review,
but here and there a few details may have slipped by.
Let's enjoy this most universal story of all."

We watch the pictures go past,
egg and sperm and cell division,

when the embryo is five weeks old
it has dark spots for eyes,
by the sixth week it is the size of an apple seed,
in the seventh week the size of a small grape,
many embryos don't survive to eight weeks,
and at eight weeks the embryo becomes a fetus,
not yet two inches long.
We watch the formation of the brain and the spine,
the curled fetus getting fed
its one-half cup of amniotic fluid per day
through the single vein of the umbilical cord
whose two arteries carry waste material
back to the placenta.
"Such a delivery system, isn't it!" says Dr. Faleen.
Even before the sense organs are fully formed,
the fetus is developing muscle tone by twitching.
"Twitching! Isn't this just the most astounding thing?"
Again, we agree, yes, it is.

"By the 24th week the baby can hear Mum's voice.
It's the voice that connects the baby to the world,"
says Dr. Faleen. "This voice interprets the world
for the baby
and will be the translator
as the baby moves out of its watery case
and has its life support cord cut and bandaged.

This voice will be the baby's best friend
and safety
in the terrifying new country."
I am determined to keep my mind on this lecture,
on this film.

The voice we hear for those months before we're born
is the only friend we have in there.
Between week 24 and week 40 the baby's brain
quadruples in size,
and one of the dangers of premature birth
is brain damage
because the baby hasn't had time
to develop its complete brain yet.
The smaller a baby is at birth,
the greater the chance of hypoxia (lack of oxygen)
damaging the brain.

We watch a healthy baby get born,
and every one of us finds some way to look
at such a thing happening,
the mom is panting, pushing,
sweating, grinning, grimacing,
crying, laughing, grunting,
torn, bleeding—

My mom did all that, too,
just to get me in her life,
and look what I have turned into.

The baby's head comes out like a globe,
not a thing moves in this room,
the midwife in the movie praises the mom
and turns the baby's head a bit
and then the teensy shoulders come bursting out
and plop,
there's the baby, wrinkled and sudden and shocked.

We've been immobilized in expectation
and now we all move our arms around,
shift our legs and relax.
The midwife puts the bloody, scrunched-up baby
on her mom's chest
and the mom smiles as if they are old pals.

Dr. Faleen says,
"Nobody fainted, good work! Dr. Moore has
toughened you.
Now we need to know the Apgar scale
backward and forward and upside down
so we can be wise decision-makers at any birth."

We get out our Apgar scale pages.
Heart rate, respiration, muscle tone, reflex response, skin.
"Sophie has already told us about Dr. Apgar,
thank you, Sophie,"
and Sophie can't help smiling
even though that was the same day Dr. Moore
trampled on her innocent question
about crumbling up on tests.

Dr. Faleen gives us Apgar problems
and we solve them in our groups.
Even with my mind nearly demented with being split
over Dr. Moore, Jolly, Annie,
the childbirth movie, and my life,
our group gets three of them right the first time.

And then class is over.
My stomach falls sidewards.

## 73.

I might never have walked toward that bulletin board
when I was 14 years old,
might never have seen Jolly's note,
"Babysitter needed bad," smudged and wrinkled
and ignored.
And I might never have ended up
walking toward Dr. Moore's office.

She opens the door when I knock on it,
says, "Come in, LaVaughn," in her tightrope voice,
her eyes like searchlights behind her thick lenses,
and points to a chair for me to sit down.
I think the chairs might be leather.
There are places to put my arms,
helpful because without them
I might disconnect and fall apart.
Hers is on the other side of a big, smooth desk
with only a few papers and a glass sculpture on it.

"I see that this lab report indicates a DNA link.
Why don't you tell me about the child you say you know?"

Dr. Moore's words are always clear,
you could never misunderstand her unchanging voice.

"Her name is Jolly," I say in a wavery squawk.
I have spent weeks not knowing
how to have this conversation,
not even knowing if it would be a conversation
or the end of my life.
Dr. Moore slowly says "Jolly,"
trying out the name of the child I say I know.
I start in, determined not to stop:
If I stop I will fall into some kind of invisible pit
and suffocate.
"Jolly is my friend, I have babysat for her."
Dr. Moore can't see through my voice to that first day,
when Jilly's nose was dripping
and the room smelled of overwhelming babies
and too much poorness,
and we didn't know how we would all change.
"She has two little ones, Jeremy and Jilly,
they are . . ." I can't bring up the words
to say I would throw myself under a truck
for these children.
I tell her their ages and that Jeremy can read
and Jilly goes to Head Start. . . .

I could tell her about Jilly sleeping with a favorite book,
about Jeremy and the Four Billy Goats Gruff,
but I don't tell any of it on this terrified stomach.

"Your friend Jolly has a husband?"
Just anybody, asking just a question.
"Uh, no. Uh, she just has the little ones,
just the children, uh— Jolly has a hard time,
but she's working on her G.E.D. now and—
Jolly has, well, she tries hard with the kids,
uh, she's got a heart of gold—"
and I have no earthly idea why I said that,
although it is true.
I want to shout till the walls shake:

> *Dr. Moore, Jolly has no idea where she came from.*
> *Don't you know that?*

Dr. Moore looks at me through her thick reflecting lenses,
thinking, staring.
Instead, I say, "The kids are so cute,
Jeremy has to go in advanced kindergarten, he learns fast,
he's been wearing glasses since before he was three. . . ."
Dr. Moore continues to stare,
not moving, barely blinking, taking it in

and I try to put myself in her place,
suddenly finding out she has grandchildren,
such a surprise must make even Dr. Moore
a little bit quivery.
"This Jolly's strong,
but you might not know it to look at her. . . ."
My voice doesn't know where to go next.

"Many women are stronger than they look,"
says Dr. Moore,
like a boat moving smoothly across water.
I don't want to hear about many women,
I want her to know about Jolly.

In the silence I read the letters
carved into the glass sculpture:
"For Outstanding Service to Youth."

"Uh, here," suddenly I'm reaching in my backpack
and out come the photographs.
I slide them across the desk, such a distance of bravery
that I am surprised at myself,
and I introduce them, "This is Jeremy, this is Jilly."
Dr. Moore studies them,
they might be anyone's children,
these smiling pictures.

I blurt, "Do you want to see Jolly?"
She can say no.
I am trying, and I'll always know I tried.

Dr. Moore moves her thumb back and forth
along one edge of Jilly's photograph,
looking down at Jilly's face
in ignorance of Jilly's personal life story.
I am wrong. The DNA report is wrong.
I was wrong to get all this started.
I should never have met Jolly.

This woman pulsing with curiosity
about her grandchildren
peers at the photos,
switches on a desk lamp to see them better,
and then
the Dr. Moore I know from lectures
looks up and across the desk at me.
When did she last see Jolly?
When did she last look at Jolly face to face?

"Yes, I do want to meet Jolly."
What did she have to do inside to make that decision?
And now what do I do?
She has said yes.

What I do is as wrong as everything else I've done.
I say to Dr. Moore,
"It would be best if you see her where she lives,
I don't think I could get her to come here."
I rush on before Dr. Moore changes her mind:
"I can take you there, I'll take you there,
I'll go with you there." Too fast, too much.

Dr. Moore looks at me and begins to read something,
I can't tell what.
"Yes, LaVaughn," she says,
"we will do that."
I look down at her desk.

I have not even told Jolly yet. Could telling Jolly
be harder than this?
YES.

# 74.

Jolly stands in her kitchen, wiping goo off the counter
and holding a G.E.D. practice book in her other hand.
"You what? No, you never. You never
found no mom of mine,
LaVaughn, I never knew you was so mean.
You get out of here," she says,
"what's wrong with you?"
She backs me toward the door with her eyes.

I say I really have found her mother.
I tell her the DNA charts fit,
and she says, "Show me, then, you just show me
them DNAs,
I don't even believe you."
I haul out the charts,
wrinkled and overly folded by now.
I show her the genetic markers and how they match up,
and Jolly says, "How do I know you ain't lying,
that's just numbers there."

"Well, it comes from a genetic analyzer,
and it shows all those close matches

between your DNA and hers, Jolly."
Her face is stubborn disbelief
and ready to change the subject completely.
I can't imagine how long ago
she learned to wear this mask
of pretending not to care.
I don't know how she puts it on so instant-quick.

I try a very soft voice.
"It's real, it really is, Jolly.
Your very own mother. She wants to see you."

"How do you know it's me?" she chops her words.
"It might be somebody way different,
it might not even be me,
them numbers."

"It's you. It is. I took some hairs from your hairbrush,"
I drift my hand out toward the bathroom.

Jolly takes a moment to identify me as a thief.
"You stole from me, LaVaughn,"
her voice rises,
"you stole my own hair
from my private personal hairbrush,
I can get you arrested, I can—"

Again, she starts to back me toward the door,
wanting me out of her sight.

Jilly comes into the kitchen
with her busy mind: "How do the people get in the TV?
Jewemy says take it apawt and find out.
How do they?"
We both look down at her. Beside the measuring wall
I can see she's already taller than her mark.
I'm grateful for her distraction
but I do not pick her up and cuddle her;
I am an unwanted outsider at this time.

"They ain't in there, Jilly,
it's only pictures," Jolly says in a tired voice,
putting the book down on the counter
on top of piles of papers and three broken toy pieces.
Jilly looks up at me to make sure.
We tall ones know all the answers she thinks she needs.
I smile down at her and I say Yes, it's just pictures.
Jilly walks away, arranging this new fact.

"I'll have you arrested, breaking and entering, you stole."

I'm backing toward the door
but I keep on. "Jolly, will you just give it one chance?

Just let her see you,
just once?"
What would I say if I were Jolly?
Would I want to find a mother who was related to me
only by cells?

"You got to be kidding, LaVaughn,
you ain't really thinking I would look in her face. . . .
And besides, I don't believe you.
You're a liar,
that woman ain't alive anyway."

But some possibility lights her eyes,
and her voice goes secretive, she looks at me up close:
"You think it might be true?"

I tell her I'm sure it's true.
"Jolly, she *wants* to meet you,"
and the WIMS childbirth movie comes to me,
the mom caressing her newborn.
"The one who had you, Jolly . . ."

Jolly huffs her breath, blinks her eyes,
puts her head sideways and looks at the refrigerator
and doesn't say anything,
and after waiting for a while

I go find Jeremy
who is playing checkers with himself.
He is both red and black,
walking around the board, taking turns.
I want to say at least goodbye to him before going.

I am almost out the door
when Jolly screams at me:
"You ain't got a dad
so you made me up a mom, that's the rottenest thing.
LaVaughn, you're insane."

It's raining.
I'm determined.

# 75.

I phone Jolly, I tell her I'm bringing Dr. Moore
to her house, I tell her when.
When she says she'll be there
I don't know if she will or not.
I meet Dr. Moore at the bus stop up on hospital hill.
We are both on time.
We look sideways at each other
around the frightening facts that have come between us.
I have eaten an unreasonable number of bananas
in the past week.

We get on the bus together and apart,
it's a wonder the bus doesn't collapse under the weight
of everything we are not saying to each other.
Our bags touch on the seat
but we do not.

Medical students say Hi to her, she says Hi back,
asks them questions with numbers in them,
"How's 807 going?" "Did you get to 913?" "Good."

I wish I were not here.
I wish I had not begun this.
When Jolly and Dr. Moore see each other—
I can't make myself face what is going to happen
in less than an hour.
I want to get off the bus now.

We don't talk for four stops.
I stare straight ahead, avoiding thinking
although thoughts are climbing over each other,
struggling for my attention.
It feels like an ice block around us,
you could look into it and see us
but we don't even appear to be breathing.

And then her voice begins. It is low,
not reaching beyond our seat.
I have to lean toward her to hear.
"If you could know how it was in those days, LaVaughn."
I turn off everything but my ears,
I keep my eyes on the metal seat in front of us.
She is barely more than whispering,
this doctor who lectures in a lecture hall.
"For every woman in medical school
there were at least three men resenting her for being there.
Waiting for us to fail.

I watched my women classmates grit their teeth,
we all gritted our teeth
trying to hold on. . . ."


I keep my eyes straight ahead. This is Dr. Moore
who has infused her stamina and determination
into all of us on Tuesdays and Wednesdays,
saturating us with courage and stubbornness.
"I would not be telling this," she is barely audible.
"I would not. Not for anything.
That has been clear from the beginning.
Only because I am ethical and principled beyond reproach
am I telling it now."
I keep my eyes away from her voice
and do not blink.
"I did what I could.
Picture the conditions:
We few women had to be better, smarter, work harder,
go without sleep more nights than the men,
they crowded ahead of us in doorways,
although the older ones held those doors open for us.
Held them open
but begrudged our passage through
into the profession we were passionate about."
I make myself look at her now
and the earth does not cave in,

nor even begin to. I watch her face,
made of cells, tissue, and blood,
and I make myself go neutral.
"I have hoped to serve humanity, always,"
she says, inches away.
"The pregnancy was—
You can't know what it was like, even 20 years ago,
such hostility in the sciences, in the medical profession—
the suspicion that we would faint at the sight of blood.
The fear that we might be superior doctors.
The expectation that we would take maternity leave,
abandon our work.
They were afraid of so many things about us."

Her posture doesn't change,
her head and neck leaning forward,
her voice so low it is almost not there.
This is more history than I had expected
and it does not tell me what happened to my friend.
My face is blank with camouflage and attention.
She leans farther down, almost hiding in the seat.
I do the same.

"When I became pregnant,
I thought at first I could do both,
be a mother and a neurosurgery resident.

311

I thought I could." Was she married?
Could I ask her who Jolly's father is?
My teeth bite down on my tongue.

"I thought I could. I hid the pregnancy
and kept hiding it,
lab coats made it possible,
and I kept hiding it." Her voice is lumpy and thready.
"I kept looking for someone to tell,
someone to talk to,
every face turned me away.
If you could know how it was,
how lonely.
The hostility, the competition."

It feels as if the whole bus is holding its breath
although it is probably just as usual,
people stepping up, people stepping down,
the bus rumbling and hissing and bumping along.

"And ever since," she almost whispers,
"in my professional life
I have known girls need someone to listen. . . ."
She looks at me and then away.
I see her back in the medical school cafeteria:

312

"Well, you'll just have to study harder
so you don't crumble up inside, that's all,"
looking into the air
and sipping her tea.

"When labor contractions began,
long before the due date I had calculated—
I had thought I had three more weeks to think,
to make plans, to figure out how to . . .
to know what I would . . ."
And here she takes a breath and
her voice gets easier:
"I was on backup ER call in fourteen hours.
I covered the shift."

My mouth opens.
My mind says HUH?
And my voice, which turns out to be there after all,
comes up: "You covered the shift?"

She unbends a little on the bus seat
and speaks fast but still so low
that no one could hear a few inches from us:
"It is possible to deliver one's own baby
in a utility room,

313

to clean oneself and the baby,
place the baby for safekeeping
in the hospital infant nursery
and cover the ER shift."
She says this as if it is not about herself.
Safekeeping.

"There were complications from the beginning.
I could see hypoxia was present,
the baby had difficulty crying,
I could see"—
she looks past me out the bus window—
"the oxygen deprivation—
and statistically little chance
for an unimpaired life for the little thing.
If she lived at all."
She keeps looking out the bus window. "If she lived at all.
I weighed what I thought were the possibilities.
Could I serve humanity
if I had an impaired child to care for?
Alone? I had no money, no—
More immediate was my full knowledge
that I would not get the residency I had applied for,
medical training would disappear, evaporate. . . ."
Her voice goes silent,

her eyes seem to focus again
on the rim of the seat in front of us.
The bus goes over a bump,
we jounce, our sleeves touch
and move apart again.

Twenty years ago
Dr. Moore crumbled up inside.

"I tried to write the date on the infant's bracelet,
I wrote 'July,'
my hand shook,
I didn't finish. . . ." Her voice ebbs away.

I should not know this. This is private
and I did not want to be such a spy
and find out how my friend got her name.

"In the hospital nursery
they would give her what help they could. . . ."
She closes her eyes.
"Leaving the infant there unobserved,
that is the one and only moment of my life
I would unlive
if I could."

She tightens her grip on the bag in her lap,
loosens it again, opens her eyes and looks ahead
to where the bus driver is driving.
Such a secret.
For twenty years.
I think I believe her.

## 76.

We changed buses twice and barely spoke,
like two shovels placed on a bus seat.
We had nearly crossed the city when she said
in that whispery voice:
"I was the first college graduate in my family.
I wanted to be the first doctor, too.
My parents worked their entire lives
to educate me. My mother was a school bus driver,
a playground supervisor, a security guard.
My father worked as a groundskeeper
for this very hospital,
and was proud beyond description
that his own daughter was in its medical school.
Proud beyond description." She holds her head high.

I'm suspended, hardly sitting down.
"Do you understand a parent's pride, LaVaughn?"
she whispers.
She leans down again and I can just make out her words:
"Everywhere I have gone—
for twenty years—

I have heard the little thing
crying behind me."

One thing is bursting out of me
and although it is the wrong time to say it
it pushes past everything else:
"Dr. Moore, I took your tea cup
for the lab."
My computer
my college education
are falling through the air,
and I close my eyes tight and wait
and wait and wait for them to hit bottom.
The lump fills my throat
and I try to swallow and fail
and try again and fail.
Outside a car honks and another honks back,
the bus turns a corner.
"It had your hair follicles in it, by accident."
I open my eyes and look straight ahead at the seatback.
"Two of them."
Dr. Moore does not say a word.

We get off the bus at Jolly's stop
and Dr. Moore steps over someone's vomit

and a smashed bottle,
just as Jeremy and Jilly have learned to do.
She steps around a broken chair in front of the elevator
and doesn't pull her jacket tighter around her.
She is Dr. Moore
and it is merely a broken chair.

## 77.

When the door opens at Jolly's place
Jeremy leaps out,
grabs me around the hips and says up to me,
his eyes boasting, joyful through his thick glasses:
"You know how come I'm strong?
Cause my arteries are growing,
you need blood to be strong like I am."
He muscles up his little arm for me to squeeze.
Dr. Moore looks down at this bumptious boy
as if he were a sudden Easter rabbit.
My heart is thwacking and wobbling and
somewhere is the best thing to say
but I can't find it and I go ahead without it.

"Uh, Jolly, this is Dr. Moore.
Dr. Moore, this is Jolly."
Everyone is at a standstill
and I blunder ahead.
"And, uh, this is Jeremy,
and—uh—Jilly, too, uh,"
I call out, "Where are you, Jilly?"
I am babbling, frantic, ignorant of how to talk

in this smudged doorway
that I have known for years.
Jilly comes bouncing into view,
pink hair ribbons wagging out the sides of her head.
"Here's Jilly," I say, my voice too high and peppy.
"Dr. Moore, uh, this is Jolly I told you about
and the little ones. . . ."
Dr. Moore looks at this family through her thick lenses
as if she has come to a foreign country.

Jeremy and Jilly revolve their bodies around mine,
pulling us into their home,
they pull Jolly and me together in a net of arms and legs,
and what Dr. Moore says
is almost not a voice, it is so quiet:
"Jolly, you are beautiful."

Jolly looks at her as she would look at a chair.
I try smiling very large.
This does not help.
I imagine the people who have told Jolly she was beautiful
and notice what the results have been.

Dr. Moore goes on in a gentle tone,
as if Jolly were not ignoring her:
"Jolly, I believe I am your mother."

Jolly looks at her suspended, hanging on to not believing.
"You are beautiful,
a beautiful young woman
and . . .
And . . ."
Would I know what to say?
I would never be in this situation
so I would never need to know what to say.
I watch Dr. Moore failing
and I don't move.

"Will you let me help you,
will you let me be your mother now?"
The mother who put her entire life
into saying two words
in a voice I will never forget,
"Breathe, Jilly,"
looks at the woman
who guessed her baby might stop breathing
or might not
and so she left her nameless in a hospital
and disappeared.

Jolly replies, "Get out."
Dr. Moore keeps on.

"Jolly, I know you can't know all the reasons,
I know to you it looks like—
If you could know how it was,
the hostility in the medical profession. . . ."
And she reaches out her hand to touch Jolly,
just toward her arm,
her sleeve.

Jolly folds backward,
keeping that arm to herself,
and she stands with statue eyes
as if they were not even her own eyes,
and the only thing moving is
her other arm, which Jilly is swinging on.

Dr. Moore's hand has nowhere to go
and it stays in the air,
reaching.
If I were Dr. Moore I would not continue talking.
She does:
"You can't know what it was like 20 years ago,
such hostility in the medical profession,
such hostility,
such hostility."
Someone in this room should change the subject.

"Uh, Dr. Moore, see how nice Jolly has Jilly's hair?" I try.
Everybody looks down at Jilly, glad of somewhere to look,
she swings among us
with her two pink hair ribbons swaying like wings
and she watches the stranger in her house.

Jolly made up a mom who loved her
and gave her everything pink,
that's how Jolly explained herself to herself.
Dr. Moore made up a self to be,
a helper of other people's daughters.

# 78.

Jilly and Jeremy pay full attention to Dr. Moore
and their mother speaks up:
"Then if you're so smart you're my mom
and you ain't a mom,
then who is my dad
and he ain't no dad?"
She is not afraid of Dr. Moore, not even an iota.
My ears go watchful like a cat's.

Dr. Moore begins to open her mouth
slowly, and Jeremy goes to her,
reaches for her hand,
and says, "You sit here, huh,"
pulling her to their torn couch
with uncountable generations of bacteria living in it.
Dr. Moore and Jeremy look through their thick glasses
at each other
and she goes with him, three steps for her, eight for him,
we watch them.
Whiffing spongies come popping out as always,
and Jeremy says, "OK, right here we sit,"

and this is a regular day in the world
and his cerebral cortex is functioning
and he has things on his mind.
"Where my mommy's daddy?" he asks.
"Where he going now?"


Dr. Moore looks at this clear-thinking boy beside her
and she says to him,
"Jeremy, he was not a nice boy like you,
he was a medical student with me,"
and she looks to Jolly and me, standing together
at the end of the couch
and says up to us, "bottom of the class,
he needed tutoring, I tutored him. . . ." Her voice twists,
tries to back up
and everything goes quiet
except the hum of the fridge.
Just out the window some pigeons coo together.


". . . He was lonely, he said he needed me. . . ."
as if she were speaking through cloth.
"Where he going now?" Jeremy persists.
She breathes out slowly.
"Gone," she says. "I don't know," she says.
Jolly takes a step toward Dr. Moore,
as if she is on her way to find him, and she asks,

"Does he know about me?"
How many years Jolly must have waited
to ask this question.

Until today I have not seen Dr. Moore have to say
what she does not want to say.
"No, no one knew," she says,
almost motionless.

Jolly's face begins to understand
and it presses on the room,
Jeremy and Jilly and I should not be here,
this should have been said in secret.
Jilly stands with both feet on my feet, hugging me,
watching over her shoulder.

Dr. Moore begins to stand up
and Jeremy puts his hand on her arm:
"You stay here, I get a book, we can read?"
Dr. Moore looks at his hand on her flesh
and she stays not standing, not sitting,
bent partly over,
and says, like a brand-new idea
that will make everything all better,
"I'll buy you a house, Jolly.
May I do that for you?

A safe home for the little ones? A . . ."

Jolly is ready:
"You think this place ain't safe for the little ones?
Think again, missus. Me, I been
keepin' them safe this whole time,
they got nobody else, I keep them safe.
You walk in here, you—"
Jolly pauses.

Dr. Moore holds on, pleading, "A home, Jolly . . ."
Jeremy is staring at his mother
and keeping his hand on Dr. Moore's arm.

"You don't know nothing about home."
As if a bird had fallen to the ground, dead.

Dr. Moore says, "Jolly, I understand—"

"Under*stand*? You should be arrested!"
Jolly doesn't blink
at this intruder bringing news and making promises.
This is Jolly.
I have wondered for years how she manages.
This is how she manages.
She is the overlooked girl from adoption picnics

and Dr. Moore is afraid, begging.
"Jolly, I want to be supportive,
why won't you let me be sup—"

"Support?
Where was you before? Huh?"
Her word "Huh?" lands like a tent over all of us.

Dr. Moore's eyes don't have the answer in them,
but her right arm moves again,
the one Jeremy is not holding on to,
exactly the way I saw it that day in the lecture hall,
genetically linked to Jolly's right arm,
and she puts her hand on her hair for an instant,
brings her hand down, open to all of us,
as she would in a lecture
to demonstrate a point about the endocrine system
and she says,
"I am here now."

Jolly points:
"That ain't enough.
Go out that door there
and don't come back. LaVaughn, you don't do nothing
but bring trouble to this house,
look what you done to my kids—"

I am out of ideas.
I unlock the three locks on the door,
hold it open for Dr. Moore,
she puts one foot on the door line and turns,
and she asks,
"You might change your mind, Jolly?
You might? Your dear children . . ."

Jilly hurtles through, holding up three fingers
against Dr. Moore's stomach,
and announces, "I'm this many."
I'm not sure Dr. Moore knows what she means.
Jeremy says to Dr. Moore's eyes,
"You go out then you come back tomorrow, OK?
We can play checkers?"

The door closes behind us.

Walking along the dim hallway
Dr. Moore is wobbly, just a little.
I keep her in sideways view
although we do not look at each other.

Outside the building, she leans on the wall,
takes a cell phone out of her bag,
it falls when her foot

catches on the broken sidewalk,
she squats, picks it up,
wobbles down again when she stands,
and orders a taxi. She has to say the information twice,
her voice lopsided and raggedy,
her hand flat over her forehead.

I say I'll ride the bus;
my mind is alarming me
that if I'm with that woman for one minute more,
if I touch the air between us
I could be electrocuted.

## 79.

Although staying away from Jolly for days
would be easiest,
I don't. When Jilly won't stop whining to let me in
Jolly opens the door. I tell her about the hospital,
about Dr. Moore as a medical student,
how she was alone in childbirth,
about the trouble with breathing,
how she was so worried about her baby,
how she placed her in the hospital nursery
for the best care they could give her.

I don't know how to say any of it.
I leave out the part
about her name coming from the crooked word "July."

Jolly is steely. "So I was sposed to die," she says.
Is this the worst news anybody could give anybody?
My hands start to move,
I watch them, they drop.

"I guess I refused.

I must of just said no, I ain't goin' nowhere.
That must of been what I did.
And the nurses,
they must of stood by me.
I bet that's what they did."

How the nurses must have cuddled this lonely baby,
must have sung to her,
fed her, changed her, played with her tiny hands and feet,
held her to their hearts,
made "July" into a happy name
to give her a good start
in a life they couldn't imagine.

How Dr. Moore must have felt,
looking at her own blood,
watching her breasts full to bursting with milk.
Determined to be a doctor,
insisting on her right to be one
and trembling scared.

I hug Jolly, who does not hug me back.
Her hostile eyes follow me out the door.

# 80.

Dr. Faleen teaches alone for a week,
I hear Dr. Moore's name murmured:
on the 14th floor, in the hallways.
Just murmured, long lab coats twitching,
eyes shifting, hands up to faces.

I go to Jolly's, mainly to check her vital signs.
She is pretending nothing has happened
and that is one way to get from yesterday
to today to tomorrow.
Her mother with pink gifts never existed,
Jolly is not who she hoped she might be.

Piled in her kitchen are boxes and bags,
across the floor, on the counters,
spilling through doorways.
Shiny boxes from stores: toaster oven,
food processor, blender,
pillows, two lamps,
loaves of bread, boxes of cereal, bars of soap,
many packages of toilet paper,
drooping heads of lettuce, bunches of carrots,

jars of juices,
avocados, oranges, pears, bunches of grapes,
cookies from France,
milk, butter, eggs,
ice cream melting in the sink.
All new, nothing touched.

"Jolly, that ice cream, the milk—the lettuce—
Aren't you going to—"

"Shut up, LaVaughn, no, nothin', nothin' of that woman.
Her and her groceries, her lamps—
Toys. They're hid away. She can rot.
Get out."

And Jeremy is singing a song that he won't quit,
even when Jolly washed his mouth out.
He just sings it softer:

> *"You can't know what it was like
> those 20 years ago,
> such hospitality in a medicine fessor,
> a medicine fessor,
> hospitality, such hospitality. . . ."*

He walks to and fro singing it.

And he has the game of checkers ready
for when Dr. Moore will come back to play with him.
It makes Jolly screaming crazy
but she does not scream
because she knows the rule:
Lose control of yourself
and your children will disappear,
become wards of the state.

Jilly has the job of telling Jolly it will be all right.
"Be OK, be OK, be OK," she says to her mom,
climbing up her and patting her face.
It is like a lullabye.

"I can't even sleep,
see what she done,
marching in here, and you, LaVaaaaaawwwwwwnnnnnn—
You are a nightmare!"

Ricky can't stay home from his firefighter classes,
but he would if he could.
"Just watch her, OK, LaVaughn?" he asks
in his sensible voice.
I tell Ricky I will make time to do this.
I drop in on a Monday, on a Friday, on a Sunday,

although she does not want me to.
I bring small books for the kids.


"LaVaughn, get going, get out,
LaVAAAAWWWWNNNN,
you don't never do nothing but ruin everything,
you ruined everything,
you get out of here, never come back!"
Jolly's voice tosses back and forth off the walls
and I turn around to leave
and I nearly trip over Jilly,
who is holding the knee of my jeans,
grabbing up at me with her other hand
that has a small plastic duck in it,
she's whispering urgently, "LaVaughn, LaVaughn—"
Almost at the door, I bend my ear down to her mouth,
and she whispers steamily on my cheek,
"LaVaughn you go way and come back, OK?"
I whisper back to her,
just we girls, a conspiracy,
"OK, I'll come back."


I get the door open
and Jolly makes sure I know what she means:
"And take your fakeysweet kissywhispers with you!"

*81.*

The note from Dr. Moore
shouts out of its envelope clipped to my lab coat
so loudly I'm afraid the girls next to me will hear it
and I rush it to the bathroom:
**Be in my office at 6:50 p.m. today.**

She allows time from the end of WIMS at 6:45.
How can I sit through Dr. Faleen's lecture
on illnesses and emergencies of early childhood
and pretend I'm normal?
But I do. I take notes, I concentrate,
I think about Dr. Moore and Jolly every four minutes.
Dr. Faleen shows us how emergency procedures
are adapted for small children,
and the room is tense in concentration
as we watch those little ones on the screen.

In spite of every impulse
telling me not to go to Dr. Moore's office,
to vanish instead,
drop out of WIMS,

go home and hide under the covers forever,
I go.

The hallways and elevator are wavery,
walls and ceilings look stumbly and deformed,
all I know is I am putting one foot in front of the other.
I knock on the door,
the lump in my throat the size of a bus.
"Come in," says her voice,
as if I were just anyone,
not the person who has disturbed these several lives
out of all recognition.

She is at her desk,
her face perfectly in order,
her eyes focused at me like arrows.
I stand in the middle of the room,
not remembering walking in.

Everything between us is out of proportion
except her voice: "LaVaughn,
I have searched,
I have ranged throughout my consciousness
seeking your motive.
Could you have been so childish

as not to sense the consequences of your behavior?
Could you have been so naïve?"
Her voice is so self-controlled
she could be asking someone to return a borrowed book.

"Jolly, her unkempt home,
her disheveled children,
her unreasoning hostility,
her inability to grasp the depth of my goodwill,
her rudeness . . ."

Dr. Moore seems to run out of things to list about Jolly.
I stand still
behind my masked face
thinking only about how we all got here
and what here has turned out to be.

It is all over for me,
it is all over for me.

"I have wondered and considered:
How you could have been susceptible
to this level of ignorance,
how you could have taken these ill-considered steps.
I can find no other possibility than this:

You seem to have conceived a humiliation
that would be both elaborate and thorough.
You set out— You set out
to sabotage my life's work,
to mire me in disgrace. . . ."


Her face doesn't change,
except her mouth
which continues to surprise me.
"A little knowledge
is a dangerous, dangerous thing, LaVaughn.
Your meddlesome adolescent sleuthing
was meticulously designed to—
LaVaughn, I would not have thought you capable,
I would not have imagined
such perversity, such malignity.
LaVaughn, you wanted to ruin me."


Blood vessels in my head feel inflated,
the bones in my skull are like metal pots, ringing,
even her desk lamp seems to dim,
the room tilts, framed awards on the walls swaying.
I stand my ground
which is shaking underneath me.

One part of my brain is still right side up,
and it tells me that this is like Jolly,
finding someone to blame when she is hurting.
I want to hug Jolly,
let her tears drizzle onto my shoulder,
I want not to be in this room.

Dr. Moore's eyes tell me I'm expelled from WIMS.
They say I have worn my lab coat for the last time,
they watch my future sliding away
and they do not blink.

"But I didn't," I say.

"Then what possible reason could you have had?
Tell me that, LaVaughn."
She believes I wanted to do harm.
She has invented this belief from thin air.

"I wanted to do good," I say.

She looks at me as a statue looks at you in a museum,
as I have seen Jolly look for years.
The air between us thickens and darkens,
I could not even swim through it.

"A seventeen-year-old do-gooder,
without the barest inkling of judgment or common sense,
LaVaughn, you are to be pitied."

Something happens,
some very small bit of open space,
the tiniest flare of bright light
and my dizziness loosens,
and although I can't explain
why I repeated myself
I did so.
I looked straight into Dr. Moore's face and I said again,
"I wanted to do good."

She stared at me with those eyes.
I turned around
and went out the door,
closing it softly behind me,
I walked to the elevator,
I crossed to the Children's Hospital,
using the open air instead of the sky bridge,
breathing long and deep as I walked out there,
went down to the basement laundry
and began folding sheets.
Find corners, force them to meet, hold them up,
shake the sheet so it pops in the air,

fold in half, fold in thirds, fold in thirds again,
add it to one of my neat piles.
The children upstairs
who are aching and wondering
and laughing
so as to be not so afraid of dying
will have clean sheets and pillowcases
to rest on.

The lump in my throat softens.
I am doing something.

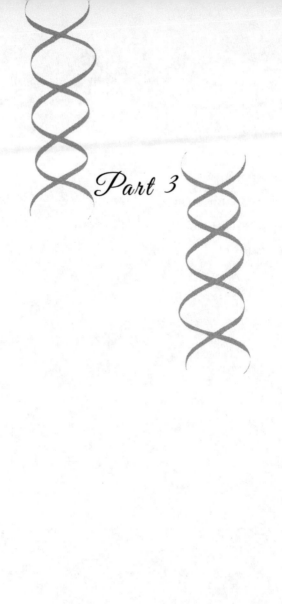

Part 3

# 82.

I unplugged my laptop computer.
No. I unplugged the laptop computer
that was not mine anymore.
I would make myself get used to it.
I wanted somebody's arms around me
in my own home at my own desk.
Is that too much to ask?
Doesn't *any*body think I did the right thing?

I went to bed
and looked at the flat, closed machine.

How much did I cry?
More than a drop, less than a bucket.

I had wanted to be in charge.
To decide what to do and then do it
and know that it was done.
Now I have done it
and the two people I have done it to
want to erase me. Eliminate me.
I think they wish I had not been born.

But what if they had lived the rest of their lives
not knowing?
And what if I had not been born?

I set my alarm clock for extra early
to go to the computers at school
and begin to get my old place in line.

I try to tell myself this mind of mine
is not the only miserable one
in the world tonight
and although I know it is true,
in here is the only misery I know the words for.
Remembering City University white with snow
I toss and turn to sleep.

## 83.

Jolly is working hard to pretend
Dr. Moore has not come in and disrupted her life,
and she is quick to let everyone know her main topic:
"I got my G.E.D. exams I gotta study so *be quiet*!" she says
every time anyone starts to sing a song or close a door
or talk.

Ricky and I watch the kids when we can.
His Firefighter Training is arranged around his job.
"Most everybody there has a job, some have night shift,"
he says, and he and I hand off the kids at a bus stop
where they say goodbye to one of us
and hello to the next one
and the first one vanishes into a bus and is gone.

My mom, who is happy not knowing
her daughter has upset the world,
just shakes her head and leaves dinner for me if I'm late.
The Tenant Council has a new group of girls
in self-defense
and she's giving all her after-work attention

to making sure they attend their lessons
so they'll learn to fight off the unexpected crazies
in our backyard.

I trade laundry shifts with two people,
I get excused from three classes at school,
first checking with the Guidance Man
who meant what he said about keeping track of me,
and every time we pass each other in the hallway
we shake hands
and he reminds me confidentially:
"We're counting on you, LaVaughn."
He has no idea how many people
personally despise me right now,
that I probably will not ever set foot in a college
after what I have done.
("All you do is ruin everything, LaVaughn!")

WIMS goes on,
I am not yet expelled.
No one seems to suspect
I am a ruiner.
After lying awake for most of three nights
looking at my weeping willow and the nest and its birds,
watching the streetlight flickering the draping leaves,

and wondering how to go on with my life,
I got it somewhat clear in my mind
and have moved to the back row.
They will have to kick me out,
take away my lab notes,
disconnect me
from my "Never Right the First Time" lab team,
unclench my name badge from my hand
in order to get rid of me.
The laptop is still on my desk in my bedroom,
waiting to go away.
And I got "Great job, ~~LaVerne~~ LaVaughn! (Oops!)"
from Dr. Faleen
on my childbirth quiz.
Rumors about Dr. Moore come and go.
She might leave the hospital,
some private problem, perhaps her health.

Tuesday and Wednesday each week
I have my notebook and pen in front of me,
working on endocrinology
and going on every machine tour,
trips through the hospital buildings
learning about equipment for dialysis, radiology,
microsurgery, nuclear medicine,

single photon emission computed tomography,
ultrasound, blood analysis, coagulation studies,
hemodynamic monitoring, laparoscopy—
looking at respirators, ventilators,
flowmeters, vaporizers—
"While we're operating on someone's carotid artery,
he may have a stroke— What do we do then?"
This and dozens of other questions
go on lines and in circles in our notebooks
and we walk on, thinking, thinking, thinking.
No, they will not take me out of there without a fight.
I am in the back row but I am there.

Dr. Moore and Dr. Faleen give their lectures,
and if I were a newcomer
I would not notice anything peculiar.
A newcomer would not think to ask,
"Which student in this group
does Dr. Moore never look at?
Whose eyes do Dr. Moore's eyes never meet?"
I walk up the west aisle instead of the east aisle
to my seat, I keep my eyes on my books
and do not ride in the elevator with her
nor she with me.

I have had practice avoiding people
and I bring my practice with me
into my eighteenth year.

Sophie asked me why the back row,
and when she saw my face she hugged me.
We went on with our work.

*84.*

Some things about Jolly's life:
One. Hypoxia at birth, difficulty breathing,
difficulty crying.
This oxygen deprivation
decreases production of neurotransmitters,
causing some of the baby's brain cells to die.
Cell death can cause impaired cognitive development,
lack of achievement in school.

Two. Left in a hospital by a mother
who pretended she was not one.

Three. Orphans' homes, foster care, Residential,
ward of the state.
Her every-which-way childhood,
the foster Gram who loved her and then died.
Hearing promise after promise
and none of them kept.
Picnics. An imaginary mother with all pink things.
Her long walk away,
Oreo crumbs sifting out behind her,
$15 in her pocket

and in her mind the common sense
to know she could go on and on.

Four. Boys. Causing Jeremy and Jilly
and then gone.

Five. Her mother offering to be a mother after 20 years.

Is this enough for Jolly to be angry about?

*85.*

I too am angry enough at Dr. Moore—
the young Dr. Moore
who laid her newborn baby in a tiny bed
and walked away—
angry enough to wonder
why in the world I am still in WIMS,
listening to her, taking notes:
"A malignant tumor can shed cells
into the bloodstream. . . ."
I write it down and she goes on,
looking everywhere but at me.

A different sort of person would march
straight from this seat in the back row
to where Dr. Moore is standing,
would make a stone fist,
aim it at her face
and watch her flesh distort on impact,
would watch her spine begin to bend and lurch,
her glasses fly off,

her arms flip and her eyes roll,
hear the slight whish of her lab coat,
see her crumple, contorted and crunched on the floor,
her name badge swaying,
her neck veins bulging,
her legs and feet settling askew, lying still.
And would stand there and watch.
Another person might do that.

I sit in the back row, my legs crossed.
"The left cerebral hemisphere
has 186 million more neurons than the right hemisphere,"
says Dr. Moore with her science voice
and her smile.
I look at her smile and I see only that it is tired.
As if it has worked so hard for so long
and wants to rest.

I imagine how satisfying it would be
for the moment
to injure her,
see her sprawled flabbergasted on the floor
confused about how she got there
and guessing at what to do next.

I sit clenched in the back row
with my unmoving face
and write:
"186,000,000 mr neurons lft cerbr. hemis."

## 86.

When Myrtle and Annie hear the news,
all about Jolly and the DNA tests and her lost mother,
they blink and gulp,
just as anybody would. Their jaws go forward,
they form their opinions fast.

Myrtle: "That high-up person, that doctor,
she did the lowest thing.
She's disgusting."

"Yeah," says Annie,
weary from carrying such a huge belly
full of somebody else's life.
"And low."

My mom's aunts made Annie's baby a quilt
with squares cut from dresses, tablecloths, curtains
through the years.
"A little thing needs a cozy quilt,
Lord knows life's hard enough,
that Annie used to be such a *nice* girl."
Aunt LaVaughn says the judgment for both of them.

My mom and I helped, matching and stitching patches
from Aunt Verna's blue dress with polka dots
and my mom's eighth-grade graduation dress:
small remembrances of the past
so this baby will not have such a haphazard life
to start out in.

They stuff this reminding quilt
from their pillowcases full of dryer lint.
These wise women save everything, thinking ahead.
It seems like such a simple thing: Thinking ahead.

I want my life to begin over again,
I would not do it the way I have done it.
I would somehow figure out a way to think ahead.

## 87.

One night my mom says Patrick called.
How to explain all this to him?
He took the time, he used his science smartness,
got us into Molecular Biology Lab C,
did what I couldn't do myself.

"He's the boy gave you those flowers
that time, your birthday?
With the foreign names
nobody in their right mind could read?"

I say yes, he's that boy.

How to tell him how it has turned out?
I'll call him later,
if I ever understand it myself.

## 88.

And then Ricky announces about Jeremy:
"This boy can read words,
but he never hit a ball with a bat,
we gotta change that."
I was to be at Jolly's by 8:00 a.m. on a Saturday,
but when I get there
Ricky's training class has been delayed
so he brings out a lightweight ball,
a small lightweight bat,
and a batter's helmet to fit that little head I love so much,
and we are going to the park.

Jolly says, "I'm his mother,
I have to be there if he hits a ball,
I'm goin' too."

So she carries a book to study if she decides to study,
she won't look at me or talk to me,
she keeps at least one child between us,
we all walk in a bunch on such a clear morning
with such blue sky
it seems everybody in the world

should have some hope today. Some. Small.
One addict even smiled at us as we passed by.


Jeremy figures out front and back of the helmet,
and Ricky begins to show him how to hold the bat.
So far, so good.
But Jeremy has a hard time finding the ball in the air
and the bat doesn't get near it. Not even near.
Maybe it's his eyes? His glasses?
Pitch, swing,
pitch, swing,
pitch, swing.


Ricky won't quit.
We all wait, hours it seems,
Jilly making dolls out of sticks,
naming them,
tucking them warm in her pockets
while Ricky keeps throwing slowly
and Jeremy keeps swinging and missing slowly.
He smiles, he frowns, he concentrates, he frowns.


"Do it again. That's 19," says Jeremy in his math voice.


I'm embarrassed for Jeremy,
and Jolly says, "He's only 5 going on 6,

he's tryin' so hard,
they should quit,
look how Jeremy's tired."
She says this to Jilly, making it very clear
she is not speaking to me.
But those boys don't quit.
Pitch, swing,
pitch, swing,
pitch, narrow miss, pitch, miss wide as a hallway,
pitch, swing.
Neither of them gives up.

"Do it again. That's 27," says this 5-year-old.

Jilly begins to jump in the sunshine,
shouting "Ouch! Ouch! Ouch!"
raising little flurs of dirt.
"Ouch! Ouch! Ouch! Ouch!" she squeaks
at the top of her cheerful lungs.

What is so ouchy? I ask.
"My shadow don't want to be jumpted on,
it huehts him," she explains,
and continues jumping on her jumping shadow.
"Ouch! Ouch! Ouch!"

Papers blow over and around the dirt.
I find a string in my pocket
and start doing cat's cradle with Jilly
and we concentrate on the string
but keep looking up
every time Ricky says, "Good try, Jeremy,"
and "You'll get there."
The air begins to get colder,
Jolly wraps her scarf around Jilly's pants
to keep her from shivering.

And Jeremy does get there.
I don't know how. It was a little soft bump,
I had just looked up from the cat's cradle
to glance at Jeremy in his thick glasses and his helmet,
and I saw it happen.
We all saw it happen.
The bat hit the ball,
the ball changed direction,
like a fledgling bird not intending to go very far,
up in the air
high as my head,
and down to the dirt, bouncing along
while we all watched.
His bat swung on around in a slow arc,
Jeremy saw the ball hopping along the ground,

studied its velocity,
curious but too surprised to be proud yet.
We cheer, we make noises, we move, we surround him,
four people crowding around one kindergarten child,
hugging and admiring.

Does this change Jeremy?
For the adults, yes.
Jolly even forgets she isn't speaking to me,
her excitement carries her away,
and even temporarily forgets that I've ruined her life.

And the lump shaped in my throat
the moment the ball swooshed into the air,
a tiny memory motion coming up from childhood,
explaining why my dad and I
have matching baseball caps in that picture.
My dad might have taught me to hit a ball, must have.
It has waited to be noticed all this long, long time.

# 89.

Why did Jody and I end up in Hallway F that afternoon,
near the southeast block of lockers just outside the gym
which is locked so people won't steal the basketball hoops
and unscrew the bleachers?
Why did we begin our conversation there?

We had both stayed very late after school for math,
most of the building was locked for the night,
we were going to walk to the bus stop.
The topic was Jody's swimming scholarship
to City University,
and I was able to say "Congratulations"
without shrinking
around the horrible things I had done
making college impossible.

Walking along that hallway
with Jody's beautiful self, his swimming scholarship,
envy pacing through me on its own,
it was just chance, not on purpose
that we stood right there right then.

He is saying how many other swimmers
tried for scholarships
and we hear— What name would I call it?
A scream, yes.
But more. A moan-shriek,
shrill, muffled, not clear
but not unclear,
our eyes go alert like animals' eyes.
At our school everyone's muscles are trained
to go taut with the first warning.

It goes away.
We don't move.

Again, a raging shriek,
we run. The girls' locker room.
Jody pulls the door open
and the scream deepens and on the floor
is— Oh, why didn't I keep my eyes on Annie?
She is spread like a cricket,
on all fours, as if she would crawl
but she is only swaying
in the position from her exercise class.
Her skirt is soaking wet,
her backpack is on the floor,
one handle of her favorite jump rope

sticking out.
She is wild-eyed, unfamiliar,
her head on a bench,
She is a stream of howling vowels.

I get down on the floor with my head against hers,
"Oh, Annie, oh, Annie, oh, Annie," I seem to be stuck
with only these words,
nothing more.

"Your water's broke, Annie," says Jody in a soft voice.
"I'm here. Me and LaVaughn are here,
you'll be OK, we're with you,"
and he grabs at my jacket.
"Feel best that way, on your knees, Annie?
Good, good, good," he rubs her back, back and forth,
"This is a big one, you're doing fine, Annie,
just fine, *good*, Annie, good, Annie, good,
you're doing fine."

I have never heard this storming voice in Annie before,
it booms off the walls, loops in the air.
Jody's putting my jacket over her shoulders,
I'm watching wide-eyed
the first labor contraction I have ever seen in real life.
"Towels, LaVaughn," he says.

Some days this room has towels,
some days not. Today, yes.
I leap,
I bring a stack of them
and Jody says, "No, more than that. A lot."
He strokes Annie's sweating forehead and he says,
"All the towels, every towel.
No. Save two. Save three. No, save four."
His EMT voice.

I do it. And I get the first aid kit that is always on the wall,
in it there isn't much. One pair of sanitary gloves.
Gauze pads, adhesive tape,
a small bottle of povidone-iodine.
One eensy pair of scissors.

Annie moans, trying to change everything.
Jody jumps up, runs to a sink, washes his hands,
runs back to spread the towels in layers under her,
I pass him the gloves. He doesn't put them on.
She stays on her hands and knees, rocking back and forth
on the thick cushion of towels.
"LaVaughn, get my cell phone,
in there," he points to his pack,
"go call the paramedics, it won't work in here—"
I go to his pack, the next contraction comes fast

and Annie is hoarse with effort: "Earthquake!" she says,
"Oh, dear Jesus God," she says,
and from the childbirth movies I have a glimpse
of what she means.

"Wait a minute," says Jody.
"She needs food, water,
she's burning calories like crazy, what've you got?"
Me, nothing but a bottle of water and two bananas.
I go for Annie's backpack, lying under a sink.
Two nutrition bars. Raisins and carrots in a bag
with Myrtle's note,

   YEA ANNIE!

I take everything in my hands and hold them out to her.
She points to a banana, I peel it, she takes a bite,
she closes her eyes.
"Give her water," Jody tells me. I tip her head up
and she sips.
And another contraction comes,
Jody rubs her back,
sweat drops slide down her face,
she is saying, "Jesus, I know you're here,
Jesus, I know you're here,
Jesus, I know you're here. . . ."
Is anyone counting time between contractions?

I don't think so. There isn't much.
I run out the door with his phone,
leaving Jody with Annie
who went to meetings about getting rid of gays,
and is grabbing him around the knees and howling.

I call 911. Of course the phone won't work.
I run the whole hallway, stopping at every intersection,
no cell signal anywhere. Our school has nine pay phones,
and the three I try are broken,
and I ran those empty hallways shouting,
and then got to a window,
911 answered
and said they'd come to the girls' locker room,
we probably wouldn't have time to go anywhere else.
I started to say,
"But her doctor is over at the—"
They reminded me
how to start the baby breathing on its own:
"You dry the baby good to warm it up,
if it doesn't breathe when you're drying it,
you flick one finger against its heel,
one finger only. Did you hear me?"

I say Yes and I run back the way I came.
Through the door there are sounds,

Annie is squatting now, over the cushion of towels,
our jackets on the bench at her back,
she is screaming, "I can't, I caaaaaaaaaaan't,
I caaaaaaaaaaan't!"
Jody tells her yes, she can,
and he rubs her back harder now,
and I want it not to be Annie
having to do this,
in my irrational state of mind I hope it can be
anyone but Annie.

She leans back against the bench.
I am speechless when this baby's head
stretches Annie so appallingly,
I want to ask God why this has to be this way,
I take over rubbing her back, hard,
Jody puts on the gloves
and puts out his hands
for the safe landing of this child,
and he's saying, "Good, Annie, good, Annie,
one more, *good*, Annie, you're a mom, Annie,
good, Annie, one more, Annie,"
and Annie is panting like a dog,
just the way I saw in the movie,
". . . good, Annie, more, now, now,
I have the baby's head, Annie,

good, Annie, *good*, Annie,
here it—here she—*IS*!
Annie, you have a daughter! Annie, you did it,
you did it, you have a baby girl, Annie,"
Jody is holding the bloody baby
who has oozed into his hands.
"Thank you, God, thank you, God, thank you, God,"
says Annie,
and she sees her baby's face for the first time
and the baby says hello in her peepy, inexperienced voice,
I wipe Annie's forehead with a wet towel,
I don't think she knows it's me
or doesn't care,
she grabs toward Jody's hands, reaching and reaching.

## 90.

Jody looks at the umbilical cord,
at me, back at the cord,
and lifts the fragile girl, bloody and hollering and alive,
cord and all,
he lays her on Annie's abdomen,
Annie puts one arm around her daughter,
she looks at the squinched-up face
of this brand-new child
with her brave scream
and Annie's tears come shining,
dropping in bright chains.

In this baby's soft spot her pulse is ticking.
I think she has a good Apgar score:
I listen to her heartbeat with my naked ear,
I take her brachial pulse,
she is breathing plain as day, plainer, in fact:
No one has ever shown her how to do this
and she figures it out.
And such a cry. She screams at the locker room ceiling
and who wouldn't? Her eensy hand grips my finger,
her legs are kicking like a dance—

yes, a dance of arriving.
She is perfect and we tell Annie that,
this mother and this smeary, bloody baby,
still held together by the cord,
I look away from their privacy.
Jody's hands in those gloves
are resting, palms up,
on his thighs where he is kneeling on the bloody towels.
I never knew. Not even a glimmer.
Not even a hint of an imagining.
"Thanks be Almighty God," Annie murmurs
and I nod my head and I see sideways
Jody is nodding his, too.
How could we not?
Four people are crying
and one of them is not even 2 minutes old.
And about the question of Is this ridiculous? No.

And in come the paramedics.
They are clear and kind,
they wrap the placenta,
they clamp and cut the umbilical cord,
they praise all four of us,
they admire the baby,
they lift Annie and her daughter gently up and away.

## 91.

At the hospital everyone turns up:
Myrtle stunned and staring through a bouquet of flowers,
Annie's mom crying into a different bouquet of flowers,
Annie's sister upset by not being there for the birth,
my mom, Jody's mom,
balloons everywhere, teddy bears,
everyone cheering for Annie,
who is not even trying to stay awake,
everyone pretending to whisper
but almost shouting, voices competing
over how beautiful the baby is,
how brave Annie is,
how she needs her rest.

"Who delivered this baby?" they ask,
and I tell them, over and over again,
and Jody says he's had emergency training,
"I was there, that's all,
Annie did the work."
He told me under the crowd sounds
he never delivered a baby before.
We roll our eyes together,

we are still shocked together,
we have blood on our clothing.

I ride home on the bus with Myrtle and our moms.
Between everyone talking at once—
". . . that little tiny face—"
"Annie—she looks different,
don't you think she looks different?"
—and everybody keeping silent,
looking down at their hands, thinking about
all the things we don't mention . . .

I know what I'm going to do when I get home.
My mind must have been waiting for just the right time.

## 92.

Jody's note. Still unread after two years
since it came with one rose one day
when I was so young I thought
it would make me break into unrecognizable pieces.
Does Jody know I have never looked at a chocolate chip
since that day?
Does he know I have never opened this envelope?
Of course not.
I would expect the paper to be sticking together
after lying in a box in my bedroom closet
two summers, two winters,
all that time, thousands of pages studied,
while my life has been taking in disappointment
like moisture.

The card I had been afraid to see
since my whole self fell apart that day
when I was too childish to know
it would ever come together, ever, ever again—
the card slides out.
It is just a card.

What had terrified me for all that whole long time
is 7 words:
*LaVaughn*
*I am always your friend*
*Jody*

That is nothing I didn't know.
Not even enough to cry over.
If I were not living this life right here
and I opened this note
it would be boring.

I shake my head.
It is the way old people shake their heads.
*I am always your friend*

And I see that my fingers are only slightly quivering
holding that small piece of paper.
Only slightly.

When I see Jody in the elevator
four days later,
we can hardly look at each other.
He lifted Annie's bloody baby
out of her body, between her spread legs,
he said, "You have a baby girl, Annie,"

he laid her on top of Annie,
we wrapped the baby in saved towels.
We glance at each other in the elevator now
and he says it's raining out.
I say, "I know."

## 93.

Annie has named her baby Jewel of God.
Her mom has added another job;
she shelves electronic parts in the daytime
and waits tables at night
so her family can try to afford this baby.

Annie and Jewel curl together
in a ratty chair with a blanket over its holes,
shadowy in lamplight from across the room,
quiet except for Jewel's small slurping sounds
and Annie humming
and as I watch they both drift asleep,
Jewel still attached to Annie's breast by suction.
This is the way it has been for so many thousands of years,
quiet, holding, glowing, slurping, humming, drifting.

Jewel of God has pooped,
it is running down Annie's arm
and I reach for her.
Annie looks quietly at her arm,
wipes it with a diaper,

crumples the diaper in her hand,
leans back and closes her fatigued eyes.

This miniature girl:
her fingers barely 2 centimeters long,
her warm bottom
so complex on the inside
is doing its elaborate processing of poop
exactly according to nature's arrangement
while her arms and legs wander and jerk into the world
and her eyes go searching for something they recognize.
She's absorbing carbohydrates and proteins
and immunoglobulins
just the way she's supposed to
and I tell her she's a good girl for doing so.

Clean diaper, clean blanket,
clean baby
just wanting to know where she is
and what she's to do here,
she breathes in my face
and I know how lucky I am.

And Gary:
Nowhere to be seen. Am I the only one angry at that?

I raise the blunt question
as soon as Annie opens her eyes:
"Annie, why would Gary just leave?"

"I don't know, he must of thought
it was God's will."
Annie looks at me with her eyes unmoving,
almost like those stationary eyes of Gary.
But Annie's eyes appear to be resting
from tiredness. Gary's eyes looked
as if he liked them fine just the way they were
and wasn't going to move them for anybody.
The only thing that moved was Gary.
Away.

"God's will? To get you pregnant
and disappear? What kind of God's will is *that*?"
I could hold it in, but I don't.
Was it God's will to smear threats on Jody's locker
and then break the door?

I put Jewel back in her arms,
she looks down at the eensy squinty face,
she puts her finger in Jewel's hand,
which clenches it tight for dear life.

"Angel," Annie murmurs, "Angel, Angel."
Here is this unique baby,
this adorable bundle of needing and pooping,
with Gary's DNA and some hope for a happy life
and I have asked such a question.

And I don't stop.
"Couldn't you wring his neck, Annie?"
I have wanted to say it for months.
I would wring his neck for her
except I would never want to touch his neck.

"Wring his neck?" she says, her voice sagging.
"No. No, no, no, no," she says.
She is not so much resentful as weary.
"LaVaughn, you wasn't watching.
I was forgiving Gary."

I take a moment to notice:
Her face is not kidding. "Look at her hands,
see how sweet,
I couldn't of made those hands by myself,
those are Gary's hands," says Annie,
holding Jewel's hand as if it were a butterfly.
"If he wasn't there

I wouldn't have Jewel,
the Angel of my life," Annie says.

This Jewel, the Angel of Annie's life,
is the reason why Annie cries without stopping,
the reason why Annie sometimes doesn't leave her chair
for hours.
Why Annie is either sleeping or sobbing
or staring into space with blank eyes
day and night.
Or cuddling her newborn, her Jewel,
as if Jewel were an added chamber of her own heart.

I don't know how Annie could forgive Gary.
It's exactly what happened to Jolly,
and Annie looked down her nose at Jolly,
clicking her tongue over how dim Jolly was
to have babies when she was nothing but an ignorant girl.

And now look! Holy Gary.
I just don't know what to say.
Forgive Gary? Forgive him?

I reach over and put my arms out
for the baby.
Annie passes her to me,

her hands clenching and unclenching,
this little gurgly girl
who truly feels angelic in my arms.

I don't make any more argument with Annie,
I look down at Jewel's face
and my hard feelings melt.

## 94.

But I can't let go of it. Three rainy days go by.
Myrtle and I are in Annie's overheated house,
moving the wilting balloons around,
picking up used plates and forks and socks,
bagging up dirty diapers,
throwing out rotting bouquets, washing dishes,
holding Jewel.

"Annie, how can you forgive Gary?"
I let it come out of my mouth.
Myrtle thinks I am crazy to bring this up
and her eyes across the room tell me so.

But Annie is easy with the answer,
looking at me over the small heap of Jewel and blanket:
"God forgives.
If God forgives the evil people
I can forgive Gary,
and I'll get to live in heaven
where it's all gold,
the streets and everything."
I look at her and I try to imagine

how that would feel,
forgiving Gary.
Rain pours down the window,
Myrtle stands still with a bag of used diapers in one hand,
watching and waiting.

"But it must be so *hard*," I say.

She looks at me, the old Annie I have always known,
about to explain something I haven't caught on to yet.
Myrtle's arm relaxes a little,
the diaper bag lowers to the floor,
she watches.
"Sure, it was hard.
I been doing it in little bits. You wasn't watching.
It took me a long, long time,"
and Myrtle shifts her weight,
repeating with her body
what Annie has just said.
Myrtle too has often reminded me to notice
what I might not notice on my own.
I perk up my senses.

This is Annie who gave birth
in the girls' locker room
because she had to.

If Jody and I had not been there
she would have figured out a way,
would have gotten the towels,
would have encouraged herself
till it was done.
People do bite the umbilical cord apart with their teeth.
In some places in the world the placenta
is the child's guardian spirit
and they wait for the cord to fall off by itself.
Annie would have managed to get Jewel born
somehow.

Myrtle puts the bag of diapers beside the garbage,
washes her hands,
and sits on the floor beside Annie's chair,
reaches up and strokes Jewel's head.

Annie says,
"Don't you know how bad hell is, LaVaughn?
You would never want to go there,
those flames for all eternity,
you don't forgive, you go there,
Satan gets you all to himself."
She closes her eyes and dozes off.
Jewel drools on her breast,

Annie's mouth hangs open,
they rise and fall together in the lamplight.


Myrtle writes Annie a note saying we love her,
and we leave as quietly as we can.
Her sister will be home soon. We're barely out the door
and have got the umbrella in position
when Myrtle starts:
"You've gotta forgive that doctor, LaVaughn."
I don't look at her. I don't want to hear this.
"Jesus forgive those sinners
that killed him."
Keeping my eyes on the puddly sidewalk will hold her off
for the moment.
"God'll redeem that woman,
that's what God *does*," Myrtle says to me.
Then why do I have to forgive her
if God's going to take care of it?


I say, "So why do I have to—"


"Don't you *see*, LaVaughn?
It's keepin' you bitter.
That not-forgiving. See? Don't you *get* it?"
Her belligerent look

is not a look you want to stare back at.

The bus comes, we sit down
and lower our voices.

"But it's her *fault*," I argue. "Here's Jolly,
left alone, *aban*doned,
she barely stayed alive, she—"

"Nobody's arguing that, LaVaughn.
Sure, that doctor did that.
I'm saying God don't want you to *blame* that doctor."

"And I want to know how come not.
How come not? Does God *like* what Dr. Moore did?
That's a sin. In anybody's Bible that's a sin.
If she's not to blame, who is?"
I've gotten going now.

Myrtle says, "You know what your mistake is?
You think it has to be not her fault for you to forgive her.
It'll always be her fault,
but God forgives her anyway.
By Jesus coming down
to die on the cross.

That doctor will never be *right* to do that,
but she has to be forgave."

I am stubborn. "How come?" I ask.

"So the world of God can go good.
That's why. So God's will can get done."
Someone sitting behind us says "Amen"
in praise of Myrtle.
The bus bumps along, the rain rains, we don't speak,
she lets me resist in my mind.
We are used to this, Myrtle and I.
Since the small wooden boat on the floor at Head Start.
In my memory it was usually Myrtle
who tried to keep the boat from tipping.

Before her stop comes
Myrtle takes my shoulder in her way.
"LaVaughn, you gotta force yourself.
Don't you know how hard Annie forced herself?"
No, I don't think I do.
"She did. Every day. You gotta *will* it."
Myrtle knows I don't like to hear any of this,
and she puts her head gently against mine,
showing me she gets it.

Forgive Dr. Moore?
I can't imagine how.
I don't know when I began to be loyal to Jolly,
but somewhere back there
I did.
Forgiving Dr. Moore
would not be loyal to Jolly.
Period.

## 95.

Next morning my mom says,
"Your light was on all hours, LaVaughn.
Honey, you worried about something?"
I tell her I was concentrating on homework.
It is partly true.
"What good does it do in the middle of the night?"
Then she backs up.
"Never mind. I know. I know. I know."

She hugs me and pours orange juice for both of us.
She does not know.
She thinks something went wrong with the laptop
and that's why it's unplugged. I did not lie.
"The computers at school work better for me now,"
I told her. She gave me a look.
"It's too hard to explain," I said.
I will have to explain everything to her someday.

WIMS goes on, I stay in the back row.
School goes on, Jody is always my friend
and because of what we have done together

in the locker room
we can almost not speak now.
We look at each other and look away.


The Aunts have finished their quilt
and it is folded at the foot of Jewel's crib
in the living room at Annie's place.
When I get there after school and laundry
I walk in the door and
of course I listen for Jewel first.
No sound. My eyes get used to the shadowy light.
Annie's sister has made a mobile
that hangs over Jewel's teensy crib,
little cut-out teddy bears and of course angels,
swinging slowly from a coat hanger hooked to the side.


First I see Annie,
slumped in a chair with uninterested eyes,
and then I see a tallish man,
across the room,
standing with the baby in his arms,
and in an instant I understand how wrong I was.
This is Gary, he matches the photos,
and in his arms is his baby daughter,
and they are swaying just slightly,

he shifts his weight from side to side,
looking down on his delicate baby asleep.
He is smiling and whispering,
all is quiet in this room
but for this feathery sound,
I stand still and stare.

This man whose hand is larger than his baby's head.
This baby who came into such a world
without asking or giving permission.
Her father is teaching her how her life feels.
I want to take back every ugly thing I thought about him.
Here he is, not noticing me in the room,
the horns honking outside shrink away,
there is just this baby
in her father's arms.

I breathe it in and don't move.
If there were angels on earth,
an angel might have made this happen,
this man holding this infant
as you would cradle a wounded bird,
to protect it
from everything.

I walk over to where Annie is sprawled in her chair,
and I put my hand on her arm.
Her arm doesn't move
nor do her eyes.
I put my package on her lap,
only 3 little bibs.
Gary sways gently with Jewel,
Annie breathes in and out and stares at the mobile
moving just a bit over Jewel's crib.
Just the still, calm whispering
on the other side of the room.

And then Gary lurches and bursts:
"Annie, she spit up."

"Yeah," says Annie without moving her face.

"I *said* she spit *up* on me." Louder.
He holds the baby way out from himself,
at the full length of both arms,
and I see a tattoo but can't read it in the dimness.

"*Do* something." Louder.
The baby starts to scream out her fear
and I would do the same if a man were yelling

and pushing me away from him
and I was 19 days old.
Annie holds out a cloth diaper from her lap,
raising it just an inch or two,
staring sleepily at the crib.

"Well, bring it over here,"
he says, balancing Jewel on his distant hands
and some spitup drips on the floor.
"Bring it *over*, Annie, she messed all over me,"
his voice is quite loud now.
With stiff arms outstretched
he carries the screaming baby to Annie.
I can read his tattoo, "Jesus is Love."
He lays Jewel in Annie's lap,
picks up the diaper and mops his shirt with it,
drops the diaper on the floor,
puts on a jacket from the end of the couch
and walks out,
kicking the door shut behind him.

I pick Jewel up from Annie's lap,
get another diaper,
wipe her frightened face,
hold her head up and put her on my shoulder,

she continues screaming for help
and we walk back and forth,
back and forth,
Annie staring past us.

I change Jewel's diaper, her nightie,
I tell her she's a good sweet girl,
lucky to have teddy bears above her bed,
lucky to have friends, and I start naming them to her,
beginning with Jody and the nurses,
I walk with her,
and gradually she goes to sleep again. I whisper over her,
"Annie, you *still* forgive him?"

She doesn't look up, but says, "Yeah,"
in her tone of voice that hasn't changed
in days.

# 96.

Three nights later Annie tells her views
to Myrtle and me, sobbing:
"I been doing the right thing
with Jewel here,
I been loving and diapering—
and washing and kissing.
I been burping and wiping.
Mostly wiping.
I been doing so much right thing
like the Angels told me to do, I'm crazy tired.
Why don't it make me have good feelings?"
The floor is covered with tear-sopping tissues.
Annie stops to blow her nose
and pick up Jewel who has begun to scream.

Myrtle gestures me into the bathroom with her.
She whispers: "Annie cried 11 times yesterday,
just while I was here. That don't count
the hours I wasn't."
I look at our faces in the mirror.
We are in charge of something

neither of us knows how to be in charge of.
Jewel is barely three weeks old.
Myrtle whispers,
"Annie didn't even start Jewel's scrapbook yet,
she didn't even get dressed since Tuesday."

Jewel of God yowls,
that helpless, brain-piercing yowl,
and Annie walks the floor jouncing her.
The phone rings six times,
Annie picks it up,
holds it next to Jewel's mouth,
Jewel shrieks at whoever called,
and Annie bangs the phone down.
She hands the baby off to Myrtle,
flops down on the sour-milk-smelling chair
and closes her eyes.

Jolly. That's it.
"Jolly," I whisper to Myrtle
over Jewel's tiny head.
"Jolly what?" Myrtle sways,
the baby snuffles and eases up on her yowling.
"Jolly knows how it feels," I say.

"She could help?"
Myrtle's eyebrows shift while she thinks about it.
"That might be worse?" she whispers.
"To think she's like Jolly?"
Jewel's eyes open in slow motion
and close again.
I can hear her pooping.
I go with Myrtle to the changing table
which is a chest of drawers
they always used for other things
before Jewel came
and filled up the living room.

I look around:
Piles of infant items cover every chair,
clothing I don't know the names of.
Towels are everywhere, wadded, raggedy,
Annie's half-empty water glasses
stand on edges of furniture, ready to tip over
if a breeze blows through
which it won't.

Annie has never had her own bed, even.
Sleeping on the fold-out was the way she lived for years.

Now her sister sleeps on the fold-out,
she gave Annie her bed
because of the baby.

It's so complicated I get tired
thinking about it.

## 97.

Jolly is still utterly angry and
when I began to tell her Annie was feeling bad,
she squared herself in front of me and said,
"You don't think I *know*? LaVaughn, I *know*.
You're the one don't *know*.
You couldn't know. I'm the one that *knows*."

Annie never wanted Jolly for a friend
and Jolly never noticed that,
busy as she was,
trying to do her own life.
Now I bring Jolly to visit,
another one of LaVaughn's interfering ideas.

An avalanche of new diapers falls
when we open the door.
We pick them up, brush them off,
pile them up again where they were,
and Annie looks over at us,
then continues staring over Jewel's head
at the soundless television.

Jolly says Hi.
Annie maybe answers her, maybe not,
I can't tell.

Jolly walks right over to her
and bends over to get a good look at Jewel.
"That's a pretty baby you got there," says Jolly.
Annie looks past Jolly at the TV.
Jolly leans in and says confidentially,
"Where do you hurt, Annie?"

I stand back. This is a question
I did not ever think to ask Annie.

Jolly squats down beside them,
puts her hand on Annie's shoulder,
and just with that hand
Annie's tears burst up: "My stitches.
My back, my back, my back.
I hurt"—Annie takes a gasp of air—
"I hurt everyplace."
Jolly lifts the baby so expertly from Annie
who doesn't resist,
Jolly holds Jewel to her own heart for a moment,
she passes her to Myrtle
and stands behind Annie's chair,

she pushes gently on Annie's back,
forcing her to lean way over forward,
and begins rubbing her.
Up and down her back,
asking, "Here?" and "Here?"
moving her hands, rubbing steadily
wherever Annie says.

A back rub.
None of the rest of us thought of it.
"You need your back rubbed,
somebody oughta be doin' that, Annie."
She doesn't even bother to look at us.

Somehow, some way
Jolly manages to come to Annie
five times in two weeks,
one time when I'm there.
Jolly asks her where it hurts,
Annie cries and tells her,
Jolly rocks Jewel to sleep,
brings Annie glasses of apple juice,
moves her pillows.

Annie sprawls in her chair,
Jolly says, "How about I rub your feet?"

Annie says no and closes her eyes.
Then she opens them and says yes.

Jolly puts a clean wrapper on Jewel,
hugs that tiny self
holds her hands, her feet, coos to them.
She could do this in her sleep.
I stand aside, watching Jolly pick up this breakable baby
and hold her without fear.

Sometimes I have wanted to praise Jolly and did not
because of her spiky replies,
this time I can't resist.
"Jolly, you're a pro. You could teach—"
And I stop. She is teaching. Teaching Annie
how to go from one minute to the next
and not die of being overrun
by everything at once.

"The Angels brought you here,
I know they did, I bless & thank my Angels,"
says Annie to Jolly, who does not look up from
wiping Jewel of God's round bottom
and putting lotion on it.

Jolly and I get on the bus

to go home from Annie's depressed house.
I tell Jolly she is amazing, how much she is helping Annie.

"It's OK, I don't mind," says Jolly,
still so angry at Dr. Moore and me and the world
that her eyes rave off and on,
but she makes the extra effort for Annie.
"Annie she'll help some other one."

It takes a moment for me to catch how wise Jolly is.
This is what Jolly does
instead of forgiving Dr. Moore.
This is my friend Jolly.

## 98.

If I forgave Dr. Moore what good would it actually do?
Does not forgiving her help any?
It keeps things the way they were before
when I was mad at some invisible, selfish person
who brought Jolly into the world and left her here.
Who could be so ignorant or cruel or crazy?
But she was not ignorant: first person in her family
to go to college. Same as I want to be.
Medical school. How could she be so cruel? So crazy?

In that utility room
all reasoning must have seeped away.
Was her whole body made of fear that day?

Forgiving is not a law of the land. I can decide not to.

What if that mother Jolly made up
with the pink bedroom set
had walked through the door,
instead of Dr. Moore? What if that other one
had said, "Jolly, you are beautiful"?

Offered to get them a house, everything?
Would Jolly leap into her arms?

What if my dad walked in the door,
saying, "See, I'm alive. You didn't really think
they could kill me, did you?"
Would I forgive those shooters in that instant?
Jolly is entitled not to forgive Dr. Moore.
Me too.
Would the birds on my ceiling forgive their mom
if she just didn't come back with any worms
and then 20 years later she did?
Birds don't make the choice of forgiving or not.
And these are painted birds anyway.

Not forgiving means I don't have to change anything.
Forgiving her Myrtle & Annie's way
would be making a bargain with God
as you would do across a cafeteria table:
You give God something, God gives you something back.
You agree to forgive people
who have done you very wrong
so God will forgive the wrong things you do
and you'll get to walk on the gold streets of heaven.

And then there's this known medical fact:
Research shows that people who forgive
are in less danger of heart attacks. I looked it up.
In anger, at least three things increase:
blood pressure, heart rate, muscle tension.
So I could forgive Dr. Moore
to keep my health good.
That, too, is making a bargain.

I think back to why Ricky didn't leave Jolly
and he's the only one who hasn't.
I stare up at the birds, their tiny feathers,
the branches, twigs, buds, nest,
things in their places
where evolution has set them,
the constant cell life of the tree trunk,
the photosynthesis of leaves.

Myrtle is right,
I've gotta forgive that doctor.
But not for gold streets
and not for healthy blood pressure.

I've gotta forgive her

—and my brain wants to fight it off,
this change of heart,
this hard retreat—
because it is the right thing to do.

## 99.

Monday afternoon. No hospital laundry to fold,
I traded shifts to work Saturday instead.
I come straight home from school
with Dr. Moore on my mind.
Her face is always with me,
taking up valuable space.

> **I am ethical and principled beyond reproach—**
> **I have hoped to serve humanity, always—**
> **La Vaughn, you wanted to ruin me.**

I take food from the fridge.
My mom's macaroni & cheese from scratch
is the best in the building
(she puts egg in it, for one thing, and herbs),
she takes it to people when someone is sick or in jail.
I scoop some from a corner of the dish
and eat it cold,
sitting at the table,
looking up at the ceramic vase that my mom and dad got
for a wedding present.
If I am to forgive that woman

because it is the right thing to do,
where can I begin?
I keep seeing Jilly's face waking me up:
"It's moehning time, LaVaughn."

I could begin
with that woman in that utility room
alone with her labor contractions and blood,
did she bite on towels
to keep from screaming
when Jolly came out?
Seeing the oxygen deprivation,
cutting the cord by herself,
washing her own baby by herself
in water from a mop sink faucet.

I would begin by thinking of that woman
bleeding on the floor,
and I would wonder
if she kissed that child.
If she kissed that child
before carrying her away,
a matter of life and death
sneaking through doorways
to leave her in the hospital nursery,
what went through her mind in that kiss?

Did she think, "I'll be rid of this baby,
I'll go on without missing a shift—"
Did she think that?

Did she wonder what that baby would do
without a smidgen of future?

Did she tell herself
she did not have that baby?

I put my plate and fork in the sink.
Best mac & cheese in the whole horrible neighborhood.
I take off my clothes,
placing them in an organized way on my bed:
jeans, shirt, sweater, belt. In the bathroom
I put my underwear and socks in the laundry hamper,
I look at the photograph of my father, Guy.
He continues to smile in his picture, a handsome man
thinking he would watch his daughter grow up.
I turn on the water
hot and steamy,
I close the bathroom door,
stuff a towel in the crack under it for the noise.

I hop in and I start.

I don't think about it, I just do it.
I pick up the soap, I start washing.
My scream isn't much at first,
a beginner's scream, all one shaky tone of sound,
just "Aaaaaaaaaaaaaaaaaaaaaaaaa."
This is not enough for Dr. Moore.
Her face spreads large in my mind,
taking such interest in her girls
caring about girls' futures, girls' hopes
and up comes a better one.
"AAAAAAAAAAaaaaaaaaaaaaaaaaaaaaAAAAAAA!"
My chest is frightened
but I go on.
I see her hands carrying her texts and tools,
stethoscope hanging from her neck
to listen to the human heart.
One hand waving down the hallway
to a group of her WIMS girls, the ones
"who will be left behind
if we don't take special care—
the ones who have to be twice as quick,
twice as clever,
twice as wise," her eyes encouraging us all:
"Treat your lives with the finest intelligence,
the most careful caring, girls."

I let out another one:

"AAAAAAAAAAAGGHHHHHHHHHH!"

And it won't stop:

"AAAAAAAAAAAAGGGGGHHHHHHHHHHHH!"

And now I'm getting my fine intelligence into it:

"OOOOOOOOOHHHHHHHAAAAWWWW!"

and my most careful caring:

"EEHHHHEEEEEEEEHHHHHHHHHHHEEEEEE!"

girls.

"AAAAAAAAAAAAGGGGGGGGHHHHHHHHH!"

My teeth ache and
I am shocked at my sounds.
Those screams should be enough,
my body is so surprised by them.
No. Jolly comes into my mind,
the way I first met her,
when she had run out of people to depend on
and those babies were dribbling up, down and sideways,
none of the three of them knowing where to turn
but turning there anyway.
I see Jolly's face looking at me
that first time,
without a clue about a mother anywhere.
She didn't know how to spell anything,

could not have read the word "courage"
on a page of paper,
would not have known it was her very own word.

I'm soaping my face and
up comes another one,
burbling the water.
"OOOBLBLBLBLOOOOBLBLBLBLUUUUOOO!"
I am screaming for Jolly,
I am screaming for Jeremy,
"AAAAAAAAAAAHHHHHHHHHAAAA!"
I am screaming for Jilly
whose own mother saved her life.
"OOOOOOOOOOOOOOHHHHHHHHHHHHH
AAAAAAAAAAAAAHHHHHHHHHHHHHHHH!"

My throat scrapes with pain,
my stomach aches,
my legs are shaking.
And I'm still mad,
I could still scream more,
but what for?
I've screamed for all of them.
Water and suds slide down my body,
blob shapes of bubble clusters,

and I scream for me—
"EEEEGGGGGGGGHHHHHHHHHEEEEEEEE!"
for how I got twisted up in the whole thing,
how I was the one finding Dr. Moore,
finding who she was,
bringing her back to her own life.
"AAAAAGGGGGHHHHHHHHHHWWWWWW!"

I could have pretended
I did not see Dr. Moore's arm move
the way Jolly's arm moves,
I could have told myself I was not seeing
Jolly's eyes, the way they look and dart,
the way she can stare. I could have pretended
her mouth, the way it says S's and Z's
did not appear to be in Dr. Moore's face
when she lectured.
"EEEEEEGGGGHHHHHHHHWWWWWW!"

How mad I am
how unfair it all is
how my future is destroyed
because I tried to do the right thing,
how sorry I feel for myself.
"OOOOOOOGGGGHHHHHHHHOOOOOOOO!"
How I don't want to forgive her.

"AAAAAAAAHHHHHHHHHWWWWWWWW!
AAAAAAAAAAHHHHHHHHWWWWWWWW!"
How I have to
whether I want to or not.
Because it is the right thing to do.
How Myrtle & Annie forced me to bring up
what I knew down deep
but would have kept down there,
pretending I didn't know it."EEEEEEEEAAAAAAAAA
AAAAAHHHHHHHWWWWWWWWW!
EEEEEEAAAAAAAAAAAAAAAAHHHHHHH
WWWWWWWWW!"
The Guidance Man: "You know the difference
between right and wrong,
and you act in accordance with your conscience,
using that insight."
"OOOOOOOAAAAAAAAAWWWWWW
OOOOOOOOOAAAAAAW!"

My saltwater tears blur into the suds
and the hot water keeps hitting me
and I keep crying
for such a long, long, long time
till I am cried out
and my hands and my brain are prunes.

In all the crying
I hear Myrtle & Annie,
knowing the right thing to do
and teaching me. From their club.
Oh, LaVaughn.

I turn the water off,
wobble out of the shower,
open the bathroom door to let the steam begin to escape
and there is such pounding
on the door of the apartment,
such shouting,
I jump.
I quick grab my mom's bathrobe from the door hook
and run.

It is a Tenant Council woman's voice—
"Is it a murder?" she bellows.
I open the door. "Who's hurting you?" she shouts,
my mom's friend who volunteers for patrol duty
when she gets laid off from a job,
glaring at me with furious eyes.
"You're alive!" she shouts.
"LaVaughn, you're OK?" she shouts.

I look at her.

"Answer me, LaVaughn. You are OK?"
I nod my head. "I'm fine," I say
in a croaky, scratchy voice.

"You have the whole building scared to death,
what is going on?"
Her body vibrates with how angry she is at me.
Water shakes out of my hair,
her voice is calming down.

"I was screaming in the shower,"my voice scrapes.
She stares.
"Just screaming," I say, softer.
She doesn't believe me,
but her shoulders give in.
She shakes her head. "Oh, LaVaughn. You."
She puts her arm against the door,
walking right past me. "Let me use your phone
to call off the alarm."
I let her walk through to the phone,
she picks it up, calls somebody,
says, "It was just LaVaughn,
Yeah, yeah, yeah.

No, cancel it, no, it was just LaVaughn,
Yeah, I know,
Yes, I know that,
but it was just LaVaughn.
No, she's OK. She is.
I know. Yeah. I know. OK."

She hangs up the phone and gives me a look.
Wait till your mom finds out is what the look says,
but I didn't need the look to tell me that.

The truth is
I am forgiving Dr. Moore a little tiny bit.
A micromilligram of forgiveness
from me to her.
For today.
That is progress.

*100.*

Not much steam is left in the air
when my mom comes marching through the door,
home from work:
"I thought I would have a little supper,
put my feet up, and
now *this*."
It can be like having a truck in the kitchen,
even when she's standing still.
"What were you *think*ing, Verna LaVaughn?
Standing in the shower and
*scream*ing?"
Her voice can shrivel a person's opinions.
I am not even close to ready
for her to find out all the other things,
much worse than screaming in the shower.
But she is here and she is watching and listening.

I begin with "You know how Jolly moves her arm up
to touch her hair—this way?"
I show what I mean with my hand.
"And how she huffs out her breath when she's frustrated?

You know how Jeremy can read all those words
and he got put in Advanced Kindergarten?"

My mom has heard more about Jolly in four years
than she thinks she should have to,
and she tolerates but she doesn't enjoy.
She reaches into the fridge,
pulls out the macaroni & cheese,
lifts the lid,
sees the hole I've dug in it—
"LaVaughn, can't you leave *any*thing alone?"

I should have thought more carefully
before I invaded supper.
"I guess not," I say,
and I tell her I'm sorry.

"Sorry is not enough.
LaVaughn, you don't appreciate.
You just *don't appreciate*."
She makes a medium-large mom-sigh
and puts the casserole in the oven to heat.
"Do the salad, LaVaughn,
let me change these clothes."
She is always careful

not to get any stains on what she wears to the office.
It is part of her plan for my life:
No stains, no drycleaning
which means more money to put in the special account
for my college education.
Such details get her attention
because of the long run.

I rinse lettuce, I dry it on a towel, I tear it in pieces,
I find carrots and onions
and leftover green beans,
I put in a few olives,
I try to make things nice on the supper table
because things are not going to be nice when she hears.

"LaVaughn, you *screamed* in the *shower*."
We sit down to supper.
I start on how Jolly told me
little tiny fragments of childhood,
how she never knew her beginnings,
she was a ward of the state,
and the more I watched Dr. Moore
the more I began to add things up in my head—
My mom stops looking down at her food,
gives me her full attention

and I begin to tell her about asking Patrick to help,
and how I stole the DNA samples
and carried them in my backpack—

Her fork clatters to her plate to the table to the floor.
"LaVaughn, how could you *do* such a—
Did I bring you up to—
LaVaughn, how could you?"
There is no answer to how.

"I just did it, Mom. I just did it.
If I stopped to ask how could I,
I wouldn't do it, and— Wait till you hear the rest."

My mom doesn't want to hear the rest.
I take her dropped fork to the sink,
I get out a clean one,
I put it beside her plate, I sit back down in my chair.
I skip many daily facts
and by the time I get to Patrick
and Molecular Biology Lab C at the U.,
she has long since put her second fork down
and let her salad sag on her plate.

I tell her how we used the genetic analyzer,
how I carried the printouts—

"LaVaughn! That backpack of yours!"

"I know. I know. I *know*. It's a criminal backpack."
She aims her judging eyes at me.
"You're the criminal, that thing is just a bag."
She is surely right. I go on so I won't stop.

"And Dr. Moore saw the numbers,
she saw them adding up
and— And I showed her pictures of Jeremy and Jilly—
And I took her over there. To Jolly's."

My mom's face remembers Jolly's house,
the smells, the sad disorder.
"LaVaughn!
You made those people look at each other in a room."
I nod my head. I still don't know (will I ever know?)
if I am ashamed.
"This is the doctor wrote you that letter for college."
I nod my head again. Every night on my pillow
I have been trying to say goodbye to that letter
and to college, too.
"You took this doctor to look at how Jolly is in her life."
I say yes, I did.
"This is the doctor gave you the computer."
I say yes, it is.

"LaVaughn, I never." She sounds tired, she sounds old
as if these three words have used up all her energy.
And because there are no words in this room
to describe what I have done to my own life
we sit and watch the supper stains on our plates.
My mom is not a crybaby,
I don't often see tears,
and I don't see them now
but she shakes her head slowly
about what we both have lost.
"I knew you should of never done that babysitting,
that girl,
it's only brought you harm, Verna LaVaughn,
and that's the truth. You wouldn't listen."

I fold my napkin,
one of the 6 matching ones I bought for my mom
in the Goodwill
for last Mother's Day. They are green.
I think we are talking about Jolly
and how horribly I have messed everything up,
but now she starts back into the years.
"The Aunts, they told me I was too young to get married,
Aunt Verna specially she said,
'Look at the mean friends that boy has,

a boy with mean friends is trouble,
you shouldn't marry that boy.' And I did.
And he went shooting baskets with the mean friends
and see what happened."

I don't even look up at the vase on the shelf,
their wedding present,
I know every ridge and curve on it by heart.
Instead I think about the kitchen stool
where my father sat,
without ever any hunch he would be shot
at random
in a public park
by a gang shooting at someone else
and missing.

I wonder if she made this mac & cheese for my father,
this exact way.
Part of me can't stand not knowing
and part of me is afraid to know.
She looks at her hands, my hands.
"Young never listens to old,
it's always the way. Of all time."

"But Dr. Moore. A *doc*tor. I hate—"

I stop.
I do not say "I hate her" to my mom
but she has heard it trying to come out of my mouth.

"I tell you, LaVaughn,
hate eats up the thing it's in. Like acid.
You need to remember that.
You hate this doctor"—she points her finger at me—
"that abandoned her baby,
you'll be the one eaten away. You can't forget that,
LaVaughn."
She gives me time to take it in.
I know it already.
"And this is why your hullaballoo in the bathroom,"
she finally says.
"Yes," I say.

"You didn't have to do it that way, LaVaughn,
scaring the neighbors half to death."
Her voice of grieving.

The only thing that separates me from Jolly—
the *only* thing—
is my mom.
She did not throw me away.

*101.*


Dr. Faleen and Dr. Moore together
pass out our Long-Range Plan page
for us to list our lifetime goals,
now that we have had these months of study.
On both sides of me
in my new neighborhood of the back row
girls are listing their intentions:
To go with Doctors Without Borders to distant countries,
to be a Nurse Practitioner with old people,
to repair athletes with sports medicine,
to be a flight nurse,
to be a nuclear medical technologist
and operate amazing machines
including the new ones getting invented.

I write in the clearest large letters I can
the goal that has come to me during this time.
I write it so Dr. Moore will see each letter
when she reads the page:
N E O N A T A L   N U R S E.
I look at the letters:

Neo = new; natal = birth; nurse = giving the best care that is humanly possible.

Screaming in the shower did not cause forgiveness. It merely helped me go through these days.

# 102.

I scrunch my schedule and watch Jeremy and Jilly
so Jolly can take her last G.E.D. exams.
I don't expect her to be nice to me,
her mind is too crowded for that.

While I'm at her house
I throw away the rotting vegetables
that were colorful and crisp
when Dr. Moore sent them over.
I line up the new piles of boxes in corners of rooms.
One is all sheets and towels, one is a play table and chairs.
I play distracting games with Jeremy and Jilly
to keep them from thinking about the toys
locked in a closet.
Jilly makes up a new game with the checkers,
where they are people,
and she makes a house for them out of a cereal box.
I watch her inventing a home of cardboard,
the way her mother did when she had none.

## 103.

Jeremy and Jilly have new clothes
for their mom's G.E.D. ceremony. It was Ricky's idea.
"Well, nobody went when I got mine,
these little ones, they should dress nice," he explained
and took the kids shopping. A dress for Jilly,
red and white stripes. Even a belt for Jeremy
with a bear on its buckle
which he can't resist showing everyone he sees.

Jolly herself is giddy:
"I passed, you are looking at somebody
that passed their G.E.D.,
how do you like that?" She is proud from head to foot.
Jeremy says he likes it fine
and Jilly sings, "G.D., G.D., Mommy gots one,
a party, a party, a party. . . ."

It's true. Ricky wanted to order a cake
from a bakery
but my mom said, "I'll bake that girl a cake
better than any store."

My mom, who looked down on Jolly
but couldn't help wanting to help her
is relaxing her outrage
at her own daughter's shocking behavior,
at least long enough to fill the kitchen with cake doings.
She baked, I frosted,
I decorated with a tube: "HOORAY, JOLLY"
including the comma,
and "G.E.D." in huge letters
across the rest of the frosting
and I put small figures of Jeremy and Jilly on two corners.
I somehow got it all to Jolly's without crushing it,
holding it like a baby
every time the bus jerked.
Ricky got paper plates and napkins and cups
and put them on Jolly's kitchen table
for after we come back with the G.E.D.


We do look like a party getting on the bus
and I tell the driver where we're going.
"You got that G.E.D., did you?" he says to Jolly,
and she nods yes. "You won't be sorry," he says.
"It ain't that simple," says Jolly
without looking back,
marching down the aisle

in her brand-new clackety high-heeled shoes.

We get seats together in a cluster
and Jeremy pretends to hit Jilly
without really doing so. Of course Jilly
tattles and we get after her for it.
Jeremy shows everyone his belt buckle again
and we compliment him on it again.

At the ceremony my mom shows up
as she promised she would,
coming straight from her job
and immediately she wants to know
if the cake got to Jolly's
"without getting ruined."
I ask her, "Do I ruin cakes, Mom?"
and she says, "With you I can't predict, LaVaughn,
you're so big for your britches."
We find a row of empty chairs,
negotiating who sits where,
Jeremy and Jilly standing on laps
so they can see this event of their lives.
I count the G.E.D. students in their caps and gowns:
Eighteen of them, thirteen girls and five boys,
and nine of the girls have babies or toddlers.
I make myself not wonder how it happened to those girls,

I allow my innards to cheer without complication
for the climb those girls have made
up from where they had landed.

Jilly leaves my lap and roams the aisle,
I watch her reaching for the hands of babies,
some on laps of grandmothers.
Naturally, these small children are cute.
Maybe that's it?
Maybe a girl can get so lonely,
and babies are so cute,
and a girl might choose to forget what she knows
about the years of poop and throwup,
the money babies cost,
the nights of sick children crying
and the worse loneliness
if the guy is gone the next day
without a trace.
Maybe she just lets herself slip down into forgetfulness?

All eighteen G.E.D. students sit in rows on the stage.
I look around the room
and in the corner of my eye
at the far end of the back row of folding chairs
sits Dr. Moore.
I think I am having an unreal vision,

a trick of the imagination
but I am not.
She sits nearly motionless
inspecting the room
without moving anything but her eyes.
Her attention seems to focus on Jilly,
who is now dancing on the squares of floor,
counting them:
"one, two, *five,* one, two, *five,* one, two, *five,*"
and Jeremy is trying to drag her back to her right place.

Jolly is getting congratulated by others in caps and gowns,
she doesn't notice her mother sitting in the room,
big as life,
I gather Jilly onto my lap,
make myself sit facing forward,
and someone steps to the lectern.
Two people speak into the microphone
and Jilly plays with my mom's wedding ring,
turning it round and round on my mom's finger.
Jeremy, on Ricky's lap, takes his belt off
and studies the bear on the buckle,
the speakers say how proud everyone is,
what hard work each of the new graduates has done,
Jilly points her strong little arm straight at the stage
and announces loudly to the man sitting next to us,

"Dat my mommy! You gots youah.
The man whispers to her that yes, he'
and Jilly points out, "See my new dwessmmy,
After each person gets a G.E.D. certificate wishes it.
there is handshaking with two official people,
and then each new graduate goes to the micropi
and makes a short speech.

Ricky, Jeremy, Jilly, my mom and I watch
as Jolly stands up on her tall new shoes
and clacks across the stage.
I can't help thinking that Dr. Moore is watching,
can't stop trying to read her mind.
Jolly holds the certificate in one hand and shakes hands
and keeps looking at the G.E.D. she has just earned.
She goes to the microphone,
moves it from where it was
for the very tall person before her
down to her mouth level
and she starts:
"I thought I never get here.
Um.
I thought I *would* never get here.
It was hard."
She reaches her hand up to her hair
in that way that I first saw Dr. Moore do,

she pushes her mortarboard cap a bit to one side.
She opens a many-folded paper and starts to read:
"I will now thank Jeremy. He is my son
in Advance Kidneygarden.
I will now thank Jilly. She is my daughter in Head Start.
I will now thank Ricky. He goes to firefighter class,
he is here today with me.
I will now thank my teachers,
some did not think I would make it
but look at me,
here I am."

She stops reading,
turns the paper sideways,
and a few people laugh.
Jilly waves to her, then puts her hand back on my arm.
Jolly studies the paper up close and then continues:
"I will now thank my babysitter,
she done good service to my kids,
her name is LaVaughn."
My mom leans her shoulder into mine.
Dr. Moore in the back row
is taking up too much space in my mind.

Jolly is not finished.
"I do not thank those

"Dat my mommy! You gots youah mommy?"
The man whispers to her that yes, he has a mommy,
and Jilly points out, "See my new dwess," and swishes it.
After each person gets a G.E.D. certificate
there is handshaking with two official people,
and then each new graduate goes to the microphone
and makes a short speech.


Ricky, Jeremy, Jilly, my mom and I watch
as Jolly stands up on her tall new shoes
and clacks across the stage.
I can't help thinking that Dr. Moore is watching,
can't stop trying to read her mind.
Jolly holds the certificate in one hand and shakes hands
and keeps looking at the G.E.D. she has just earned.
She goes to the microphone,
moves it from where it was
for the very tall person before her
down to her mouth level
and she starts:
"I thought I never get here.
Um.
I thought I *would* never get here.
It was hard."
She reaches her hand up to her hair
in that way that I first saw Dr. Moore do,

that did not give me a chance to make it.
They betted against me
but I won. Here I am."

Jolly, who has for so long lived sideways,
walks straight and upright to her chair
and holds her G.E.D. certificate in front of her
like a map. Everyone claps
till the waves of her gown stop jiggling.
What is Dr. Moore thinking?

Some of the graduates get flowers.
Not a one of us thought of that for Jolly.

My mom lines us all up and takes pictures
in different groups. Jeremy holds up his bear belt
for every one of them.
My eyes keep sneaking back to Dr. Moore.
I can be with both kids, my mom, Ricky,
everybody congratulating Jolly,
and still watch her walk across the back of the room
and out the door.
My mom is explaining to Ricky
that she wants us all to go in a taxi back to Jolly's house
and she will pay for it. Ricky gets it
about not saying no to my mom's willpower.

"We get cake now?" Jilly wants to know,
tugging on me, but we don't get to leave yet
because Jolly has run out on her clackety shoes
saying "Wait a minute, wait a minute,
wait five minutes—"
and we all sit down again, except Jilly and Jeremy
who pass the time running between the rows of chairs
till Jilly falls down and we all comfort her
and my mom takes more photographs
and nearly everyone is gone.

Jolly comes running back,
out of breath. "Well, I did it.
I made a copy of my G.E.D. for that billionaire,
didn't think I'd ever get that far, did you?" she says to me.

The billionaire: My first year with Jolly.
She found out about the billionaire
who gives his money away
to needy people. When she wrote to him
he said first she'd have to send him proof of her G.E.D.
and then he would reward her tenacity.

Jolly's tenacity. It has lasted all this time.

Finally, we are in a taxi

which Jeremy loves and wants to help steer.

He announces to the driver,

"My mom gots a G.E.D., you wanna see my bear?"

and shows his bear buckle and the driver praises it twice.

# 104.

My mom says, "There must be a sheet in this house
not already on a bed
we could use for a tablecloth."
Jeremy pulls a sheet out of a congested drawer.
"Purple spaceships, see? Good, huh?"

My mom tells him yes, they're good,
and they spread the wrinkled spaceships
over Jolly's quite icky kitchen table.
We arrange the cups and plates and napkins
all around the fancy cake.

Ricky has buckled Jeremy's belt correctly again,
and gets two juice cartons from the fridge.
Jolly finds a knife and starts cutting,
Jilly is prancing in her striped dress
and Jeremy nags her: "Cut it out, cut it out,
you'll ruin the party,"
and I tell him Jilly is not ruining the party,
she's making it nice by dancing,
when the doorbell rings.

I saunter over and open it,
with cake saying "grat" on a paper plate in my hand.

Dr. Moore stands in the dim doorway
holding a package,
and the first thing I think of
is how she must have decided to come here.
Would I walk into a place
where the person I want to love me
hates me?
I don't know what to say to such lonely bravery
and I stand blank in the doorway,
wishes and fears trying to sort themselves
in my noisy brain.

"Good evening, LaVaughn,
may I come in?" she asks,
the first words she has said to me since
"you wanted to ruin me,"
and again she is the kind and friendly doctor
who told me I had the gleam
and I almost thought I had a hint of what she meant.

Jolly sees the open door,
her mother standing on the threshold,

me stranded with my hand on the door,
and she says, "Where did she come from?"
Her voice so flat it seems run over.

"I came to congratulate you, Jolly."
Everyone's head turns toward this reasonable tone,
I open the door wider and stand aside.
She takes two steps and is in.

Dropped in from her high place
she stands beside a bare lightbulb lamp,
holding in her hands a skinny package
wrapped in pink ribbon.
Everyone watches.

## 105.

She could have fallen like a meteorite to this spot
but she speaks regular words:
"Hello," "Congratulations, Jolly,"
"Hello, little Jilly." "Jeremy."
Ricky is pouring more juice into Jeremy's cup
which he does not stop doing.
Jolly has taken off her shoes
and stands barefoot
on the spot of ketchup
that Jeremy and I spilled three years ago
and everyone has been grinding into the carpet ever since.
"That's her," Jolly says to Ricky,
pointing with the butcher knife
coated with frosting ruffles,
"that's who left me in the hospital
and went back and worked her shift,
that's the one." Her flat board voice.
She puts the knife in the sink
and turns her back to everyone.

Ricky partly nods to Dr. Moore
and says, "I seen worse."

My mom looks at Dr. Moore,
I see the computer and college recommendation letter
go through her eyes
and, right behind them,
her view of any woman who would dump any baby.
My mom walks three steps
and although she could say
"Fine mess you've got here,"
what comes out is "I am LaVaughn's mother."

I watch Dr. Moore in profile.
She has spent years not flinching
but something in her flicks or twirls,
just a part of her neck and shoulder,
the sternocleidomastoid muscle
attached to the clavicle
that I put on our skeleton at WIMS
all those months ago.
She seems to consider shaking hands with my mom
but does not,
to consider smiling her room-filling smile
but does not,
and she says, "Oh. LaVaughn's mother"
as if she is reading from a screen.

My mom continues the conversation she has begun.
"Jolly done fine on her G.E.D. work,
and cared for these children all the while,
you proud of this girl?"

Dr. Moore appears to appraise the question.
She looks away from my mother
toward Jolly's back
and I follow her eyes.
Jolly is picking up a corner of cake frosting
with her fingers, putting it in her mouth,
licking her fingers slowly.
When Dr. Moore left her
unnamed and trying to breathe
she was barefoot then, too,
and didn't know that hand was to eat with.

"I don't have any right to pride in Jolly.
I am in awe of her," says Dr. Moore.
Her voice is unbroken on top
but her hand is quivering.
She changes the package to her other hand.

Jolly turns slightly toward me and says,
"Why don't she go away?

Don't she get it she ain't wanted here?"

The room goes silent
except for Jilly swushing her new dress back and forth,
giving us something to watch
so we can almost pretend Jolly hasn't said that.

The Guidance Man:

> **. . . you know the difference between right and wrong,
> and you act in accordance with your conscience,
> using that insight.**

I have to.
I walk to Jolly, I say above a whisper,
"You could look at her."

Jolly's voice is on the loud side:
"Yeah, I could. I could put my hand on a hot stove, too.
Why would I want to look at that no-mom,
wouldn't even claim her own baby?"

Now Dr. Moore moves in, takes a step forward.
"You are the strong one, Jolly,
you are the one who insisted on living,

you hung on. . . ." She was going to say more
but her voice stops working,
her mouth moves, trying to say words.

Before I am completely aware that I am talking out loud,
I say, "Jolly, tell her what you did. With Jilly."

"Huh?" says Jolly,
who is concentrating on keeping her back turned.

"About the spider leg. When Jilly was a baby. Just tell.
Please, Jolly?"

The only sound I hear is Jeremy breathing in.
"I pushed the 9," he says.
Everyone looks down at him.
"Jilly couldn't breathe, Mommy blowed in her mouth,
I pushed the 9, LaVaughn pushed the 1-1,
men came.
Jilly & Mommy went to the hospitality,
I went to LaVaughn's house,
we ate sausage.
Jilly's OK now, see her?"
He points his arm out at Jilly,
standing in her perfect flesh and blood.

Dr. Moore takes in this report,
hears for the first time that her daughter
saved the life of her granddaughter
who is twisting her red and white dress in her hands
not two feet away
and scattering her smile on everybody.
Dr. Moore looks down at the child, the dress,
up at Jolly, and takes another step forward.

Jolly pulls her face in and backs away,
past the cake toward the wall. Dr. Moore stops walking.
I hear my voice,
sounding to myself like a dropping hammer:
"Jolly, you had to find each other,
you could not go through your whole life without—"

While Jolly is saying, "Shut *up*, LaVaughn,
you don't do nothing but ruin things—"
Dr. Moore takes a step toward me,
looks at me hard with her complicated eyes,
and asks, "LaVaughn, what ever made you imagine—
What made you think—"
And she stops.

"I saw you move your arm," I say.

Jeremy faces Dr. Moore, holds up his hand
and begins to pull back his fingers with his other hand,
teacher style.
He counts to her, bending his index finger:
"Look. Here's me, I'm that finger.
Then there's my mommy, she's this finger,
so you get the next finger, so you fit.
Mothers in a row, get it?"
The room is waiting
and Jeremy calmly goes on.
"And there's Jilly. She goes on the same finger with me
for being kids.
Generillions. Generollions. Uh— *You* know.
Gener— *Gene*r—"


Dr. Moore looks down
at this inquiring boy's outspread fingers,
and she kneels down on her knees,
eye level with him.
"Generations," she says,
"yes, Jeremy, you're right: Generations."
Her hand is on his arm.
Jolly twitches, and who wouldn't?
Ricky's hand comes around her elbow
holding her back.

Jeremy continues. "Yeah. Generations,
then how come you don't gots your bed in this house?"
he asks his grandmother
and lets his fingers go back to their natural places.
He looks down at her hand on his arm.

Not even Jolly says a word.
Dr. Moore takes Jeremy's hand in her hand,
looks down at it, lifts it up
and kisses it,
next to the chocolate frosting smear on his knuckles.
He watches her
and he turns her hand over and kisses it back.
No sound but lips on skin.
"Wanna see my bear belt?"
He points down to the buckle on his belly.
"Your very own bear," says Dr. Moore.

I see her do what I would not do with Jolly:
She tries again.
She gets up off her knees,
she walks toward Jolly and puts her arms out.
Just that. Two arms
spread wide enough for Jolly to walk into
if she will.

While Jolly is saying "Go away, go away, go away,
get out of here, go away, get out of here,
go away, go away,
get out of here, go away,"
Dr. Moore keeps inching closer, closer,
Jolly doesn't stop, "Go away, get out of here,
go away," and Dr. Moore's arms go around Jolly
who repeats, "Go away, go away, go away, go away. . . ."
and her voice stops
as if something fierce inside her has worn itself out.
I hold my breath,
Jolly takes a step forward.
I watch her move into Dr. Moore's arms
as if she weighs nothing.

Jilly watches her mother and her grandmother
learning how to touch each other,
Jolly goes ahead and lets herself sob:
the Oreo cookies, the pink bedroom, the refrigerator box,
more cold rain and brutal nights than I'll never know,
Dr. Moore holds Jolly's head carefully next to hers,
the way you teach a child to hold an egg,
and they move, not even an inch,
from side to side and back again
as Jolly cries and cries and cries and cries and cries,

and Dr. Moore murmurs with her eyes closed,
"Mmmm, Mmmmm, Mmmmm, Mmmmm,"
and in the still room
Jilly shuffles across the floor
in Jolly's strappy shoes,
she reaches up Dr. Moore's hip
and pats her, singing: "Hello, hello, hello, hello, hello."

The unforgiveness I have gotten so used to,
gripped around my heart
where it had some kind of fear of going anywhere else,
loosens a bit, unclenching inside me,
it hovers over the place where it has lived so long,
and watches to see what I will do.

Along with everyone else
I turn my eyes away so as not to interrupt
but when I look back at them because I can't help it
Dr. Moore opens her eyes
and she smiles at me, not the lecture smile of WIMS,
a thinner, not so effortful smile.
And she says to me: "Thank you, LaVaughn.
Thank you, LaVaughn."

## 106.

As the package slipped out of Dr. Moore's hand
Jeremy picked it up and untied the ribbon
around a sheaf of papers
that didn't make any sense to him.

"What does 'benefit' mean?" he asks.
"Hey, here's my name Jeremy."
A health insurance policy for Jolly, Jeremy, and Jilly,
the first one they have ever had.

This thought spins in Jolly
and comes out through her eyes and one lifting hand,
as if she has reached some unexpected destination
where the customs and language are not the same,
somewhere she has never been before.

## 107.

At home in my bed
the hubbub of other voices quiets down
and only Jolly's accusing one comes up:
"You ain't got a dad
so you made me up a mom. . . ."
I listen slowly, I let it repeat. And again.
It was because of my own father?
*That's* why? *That's* why?
It's all because of *me*? I thought I was helping her.
But I was only trying to help me?

I look over at my dad's photograph on my desk,
exactly where I expect him to be,
beside the unplugged laptop computer.
His face hasn't changed
in the twelve years that he has stayed in his frame,
often with books piled in front of him,
often with a daughter moaning and complaining
and declaring,
sometimes with a daughter whose brain is so knotted
nothing gets said for hours.

Jolly thinks it's all because of him.
I never can ask him a question, ever.
His advice. His opinions.
What would I do if I had any choice in the world?
Bring my dad back of course.

I try to swallow over the enormous lump in my throat.
I sit up. I get a drink of water. It will hardly go down.
Then my dad *is* the reason for my lump.
He's the whole reason.
What would I give to have my dad back alive,
have him walk in the door and say Hi?

The answer comes to me
in little jerks of thought:
the computer, my admission to college:
I risked those
to get Jolly and her mother together
so I could pretend I was getting my father back.

And Jolly knew that and nobody else did?
My heartbeat must have been bursting at the seams
all this time
while it waited for me to understand.

My mom.
All these years. How she must have wanted
to do what I have done.
Make reunions between people
so she could imagine it was her own.

I cry and cry for as long as I want,
late and alone and not stopping.

## 108.

I take Saturday off. I will do no homework,
no anything. My mom is with her girlfriends
getting their minds unjangled at a movie,
these rooms are quiet, not even a faucet dripping.
All parts of me need a rest.
Too much of everything has happened,
my brain cells feel depleted.
This cannot be true physiologically
but I am too tired to take that into account.
I pour a glass of orange juice and take it to my room.

I am horizontal on my bed,
even my tree of birds takes too much energy to look at.
But my mind won't let down.
It knows this is mid-morning,
the time for thinking, working, moving.

Down in the street, cars honk at each other,
dirty words tumble out of doorways,
children holler in their sidewalk games.
I pick my head up enough to drink some juice

and droop back down.
I used to be
just a plain person eating and sleeping
and then I began disturbing people's lives
and now look.

I watch the clock, trying to catch the minute hand
moving.
The doorbell rings.
I lie inert.
Standing up is too much trouble.
The bell rings again.
I'll lie here till they go away.
I close my eyes.
It rings again. Again.

On my way I notice
my mom has put the mail on a table.
I open the door in moody annoyance
and Patrick stands there, as if he were loitering.
Why on earth has he come to this address?
He has one hand behind his back
in a raggedy sweatshirt sleeve, the way he used to be.
Something wisps and bends in the air,
not an aroma, not a sound, not really anything,

I wave it away with inattention.

"Hi, LaVaughn," he says.

"Hi, Patrick." He has interrupted my idleness,
my not thinking.


"Uh, how did the DNA work out?

The people you wanted to put together?

Did it—

I mean, were they—

I mean—" He stops, he turns his back to me,

I think he's going to walk away.

He has a paper bag in that hand behind him.

He turns around again, stands up even straighter, and asks,

"Will you go ice skating with me at Christmas?

I can make it all the way around the rink backwards."

This is the same old Patrick and not.

"Sure, I guess so. Christmas? That's months away—"

Something in the tilt of his head,

something in his constant eyes,

I begin to pay attention.

He takes a part of a step forward and stops.

"LaVaughn, do you even know I exist?"

What in the world does he mean? "Uh, sure.

Uh, what do you mean?"

This is the lab assistant in Molecular Biology Lab C
who changed Jolly's life
and Dr. Moore's
and I can't remember if I said
thank you or not.
The boy I dreamed about without wanting to,
kept seeing in lunch line, totally imagined.
Without any thought of him, he just turned up
in those odd, asleep places
uninvited.
"I brought you something."
He holds it out.
"It's nothing much."

I reach out my hand
because I don't know what else to do.
I watch his hand, the bag, my hand,
the paper crackles,
I open it
and inside is a very large chocolate chip cookie,
as if a law has been broken in this doorway.

My mood totters, fidgets, bumping into itself,
the world has been going on
since I swore off chocolate chips all that long time ago.

I hold the cookie on the bakery paper
and look at him.

> *Patrick, I can't eat a chocolate chip cookie,*
> *I haven't looked at a chocolate chip for two years,*
> *you don't know what happened,*
> *you never knew how I baked the cookies,*
> *arranged them on a plate,*
> *opened the door—*
> *saw that kiss—*
> *ran away—*

I say, "It's a cookie. A big one. Thank you, Patrick.
You want to come in?"
We both stand where we are.
This is not even what I intend to say.
What do I intend to say?

> *What are you doing here, Patrick?*
> *If you would go away things would be simple again.*

"I thought about you. Every day.
For three years, LaVaughn.
You never knew that.
You never even wanted to know it.

LaVaughn, if you got in an accident—or something,
I'd donate my blood for you."

I listen closely.
No, I never knew that.

"I even hallucinated you,
in the Art Museum one day,
in with all the statues
I invented you, standing behind a sculpture.
That's how bad it got."
He tells me this straight and clear,
no shifting around, no sudden stopping.

I am too surprised to stay still.
"Patrick, that *was* me. I was *there*.
I saw you, you didn't even look back."

He stares. At my neck. My left ear.
"Even back in Summer Science, even before that,
the way you get to caring about things,
some kind of—I don't know,
it comes out and shines or something—
I don't know,
you're the only girl I ever told why I talk slow.
I almost thought you weren't in the lab at all,

I thought maybe I dreamed you."

He thought maybe he dreamed me.

"You want to come in?" I say again
and this time I seem to mean it
because I see my arm opening the door wider.
I keep the chocolate chip cookie at a distance.
Patrick steps in.
He was here that one time before,
my birthday party,
oh, we were so *young*.

He got his face bloodied because of me.

We stand wide apart looking at each other.
I am glad his voice goes slowly
so I can take in every word.
"I'm going to Africa tomorrow
and I can't go away and not know.
Not know about you.
LaVaughn.
I brought you a cookie
and I'm trying to ask you
if—
LaVaughn, say something."

I don't move. The walls prick up their ears.
"LaVaughn."
He walks toward me and says my name
as if he has been thinking it for some time.
I haven't ever heard it said this way.
My legs go funny, I take a step across the floor
but they move like someone else's
that I am not used to,
even though I am in my own house.


I get close enough to put my hand on his arm,
I say, "I should have thanked you more,
for the lab work, uh. . . ."
He looks at my hand on his arm.
Nature has random patterns,
and it is people who put names on them.
What is the name
for how my hand feels on his sleeve?
How it feels to him,
to me?
My hand doesn't move.
His intricate eyes on my face
take my mind off myself
and I get a coating of goosebumps up my whole body.
His other hand goes to my shoulder,

to the back of my neck, like a small, warm pillow,
and our faces barely move
and yet they come very close to each other
and I could turn and run
if I wanted to.
I have waited my whole life
and I close my eyes like in the movies
and I don't know what to do with my mouth
but my mouth finds out.
I am being kissed
and waves of goodness come up in me,
even perfection.
So this is kissing.
Kissing is gradual and nearly silent,
Oh          Oh          Oh.

I open my eyes, not to miss any of it.
and I see his open eye
staring into mine
and we stay that way
watching each other being kissed,
and behind that eye is his startling brain,
and I close my eyes again,
he moves his lips
I move mine

my breath comes suddenly
in my mind I say "Patrick" in a drift of curious wondering,
my whole life seems to be just these two mouths,
my heartbeat stretches, it chimes,
this is the reason why I'm alive.
Galaxies are moving away from each other,
and this is all I want
ever.
And then it stops.
I want to wave a flag in his face, shouting
This is my first time ever! Don't go away!
I'm afraid the whole kiss will disappear,
everything going back to before. "LaVaughn," he says.
Did that kiss really happen?
Would anyone believe me if I said it did?


Our mouths are doing it again,
Patrick and I are exchanging bacteria,
a joyful contamination,
little teensy sounds,
one mild slurp,
arms are everywhere, we could not come unfastened,
in an instant
the bronze museum lovers leap through my head
and are gone,

Patrick pulls back just an inch and looks at my mouth,
almost whispering into it, "You did know I exist,"
and I say "Yes." I bring the cookie in my hand
and slip it between us.
I will take a bite of it,
I will will myself to,
but it gets to Patrick's mouth first,
he takes a bite,
holds it in his teeth,
puts it in my open mouth,
he takes another
and we chew, looking at each other
over the cookie, I swallow. I take another bite,
proving to myself
that I can.

He puts all his fingers on my cheekbones,
his palms under my chin.
"So this is what your face feels like," he says.
"I've always won- won- won-
I've always won  dered."
I nod my head yes.
I feel the most patient I have ever been.
I can wait for anything and everything to begin.
We breathe.

"You came back in my sleep," I almost whisper,
"after the Art Museum
I kept dreaming you,
I didn't know why. You were just there."
He kisses the small hollow where my clavicles meet.
"Now I'm just here," he says to my neck.
And over my shoulder he says, "LaVaughn,
there's your letter, did you open it?"
He turns me around with his arm
and the thought flies through my mind
that until this moment
I would not have let him turn me in any direction,
and on the table where his finger points
is an envelope with "City University" on the corner
and my name and address in the middle.

"Oh, no— No— Uh, no." I cannot let him see
that I didn't get in,
Dr. Moore took back her letter,
my test scores are too low,
my mom and I are too poor,
I'm not prepared enough to go to the University
and I try to push his arm off to the side.
But he picks up the envelope,
the bones in his hand

moving toward the bones of mine,
I want to slow them down,
make it happen tomorrow
or not at all,
these hands about to touch around paper.

I can't not open the envelope now.
I stand apart from him, to be alone with the bad news.
    Dear LaVaughn:
    We are happy to inform you of your acceptance
    at City University. . . .

Some squeak comes from me.

Patrick reads over my shoulder.
"Hello, college girl," he says to my chin.
"Congratulations," he says behind my ear
and I nod my head.
He says, "Look at the financial aid part,
over here—" He moves the page sideways.
The words are there, the numbers, many of them,
Patrick says, "That much?"
I say, "*That* much?"
Never in my life have I seen that much.

I am going to college.
Me, LaVaughn.

I hold the letter in my hand
just inside the doorway
of this house of everything I have hated and loved
and feared, insisted, resented,
wanted, and wanted to forget.
It's not finished after all, my thinking and growing.
I stand still and wish I could breathe it all in at once,
the unexpected taste, the weight,
the worrying, doubting heart of it,
the joy
in this full house.